LAST CHANCE SALOON

Former gunfighter Brett Cassidy now leads a peaceful life as a trapper. Then he receives a letter from Lonesome Valley, begging him to consider coming out of retirement to help the homesteaders there in their fight against a greedy rancher. Though Cassidy has hung up his twin Colts, the letter is written by Harmony McBeath, the widow of a man who once saved Cassidy's life. He owes her something for that. So he straps on his Peacemakers and heads out . . .

COLE SHELTON

LAST CHANCE SALOON

Complete and Unabridged

LINFORD
Leicester

First published in Great Britain in 2019 by
Robert Hale
an imprint of The Crowood Press
Wiltshire

First Linford Edition
published 2023
by arrangement with The Crowood Press
Wiltshire

A catalogue record for this book is available
from the British Library.

ISBN 978–1–4448–4868–7

1

Brett Cassidy reined in his big roan horse by the sprawling cemetery.

Remaining in the saddle, he looked for the two freshly-dug graves and found them, side by side, in the deepening shade cast by a lonely old spruce tree.

With an ancient buzzard watching from the spruce's highest branch, he read the inscriptions on their new headstones. One belonged to Sheriff Ed Buscombe and, according to the poignant words carved under his name, the town lawman had worn his tin star with pride and served the town of Jericho Creek faithfully for twenty-three years. The other grave was the final resting place of Amos Ridley Sporn, part-time deputy and town barber. If he was still breathing, he would have celebrated eighty-six years next Thanksgiving Day.

According to the Jericho Creek Town Committee's urgent letter, delivered in person by Mayor Matthew Whittaker's hard-riding son to Brett's lodgings in Arrowhead City, both lawmen had been murdered. They were shot in the back after dark as they left their office to walk home. The two well-liked law officers had left behind a pair of grieving widows and a struggling community overcome by fear.

The committee's letter, along with a five hundred dollar payment-in-advance for his services, sat folded in Brett's hip pocket. His professional fee was normally double, sometimes even triple this amount, but he'd made no argument because Sporn had once been a friend of his father's, the two men and their families having come west together across the Great Plains on the same wagon train. At the time Brett had been a gangling teen but he still remembered the old barber who'd once cut his hair, nicking his left ear with blunt scissors. Now both Amos Sporn and his own father, Gabe Cassidy, were dead. Gabe and Linda Cassidy, Brett's parents, had succumbed to a frontier fever almost twenty years ago and rested together in a cemetery one mile outside Arrowhead City.

Brett picked up his reins, took a last look at the graves and kept riding.

The town of Jericho Creek was just ahead, basking in the late afternoon sun. As Brett rode closer, he saw shadows stretching like long, dark fingers over Main Street. The slight northerly wind blowing from the distant mountains whispered down the alleys, raising little puffs of dust and ruffling the tepid water in the horse troughs. The town was silent, like the silence of the graveyard Brett Cassidy had left behind.

Brett eased his tall, rangy frame from the saddle.

He was a man in his early forties. You wouldn't call him handsome, but he was a man most women would look at twice. Many searing suns and freezing winter winds had chiselled his face. He had high cheekbones, a prominent nose, thin lips and a jutting jaw that warned all and sundry that he wasn't a man to be trifled with. There was a small scar to the right of his mouth.

Now at trail's end, he secured his roan to the tie-rail fronting The Buffalo, the town's one and only saloon, which stood alone like a beacon on the dusty hillock overlooking Main Street.

Taking his time, he let his gunfighter's cold, dark-brown eyes rove over Jericho Creek. The vast forest that sprawled over the western ridge had provided the wood for the street's clapboard-fronted business houses, log cabins and board-walks — and also the pine boxes that lately had been lowered regularly into the clay soil. Usually, Main Street was bustling with life. Most late afternoons, women in frilly bonnets and long skirts were still shopping, children were play-ing hopscotch and men could be seen yarning with Blacksmith Blake by his forge, but today the street was deserted.

The townsfolk were mostly safely indoors.

They knew what was about to happen

because Whittaker's son had ridden back ahead of Brett. Unable to keep his mouth shut, a common failing of his, he blurted out impetuously that the town was about to be set free, courtesy of the territory's fastest gunfighter.

Brett was in no hurry.

He just kept looking over the town stretched out below him. The Procter boys, Wolf and Dale, would be holed up down there. Despite killing two lawmen, they weren't the kind to run. Not the Procters. Doubtless they'd heard the word Brett Cassidy was coming, so they'd be waiting for him, boasting to all and sundry they could take him when the time came.

He lifted his guns, twin dull blue Colt Peacemakers, checked them both and slid them back into their brown leather holsters. They had been hired before, ten times in fact, and each time they had killed. The first time had been in Grizzly Pass when he'd gunned down a hardcase named Logan; the last in a high country camp where he'd caught up with Mossman, on the run after raping and murdering a rancher's new wife. Although Brett Cassidy was a hired gunfighter, he'd never been a man to carve notches in his guns, but he remembered each killing, each man to fall, each life ended by his deadly Colts. And soon his tally would become twelve, maybe more, he couldn't be sure right now.

'Mr Cassidy . . . Mr Cassidy,' he was summoned from the other side of the batwings. 'It's Mayor Whittaker.'

The voice was high-pitched, excited, plunging the saloon into silence.

Brett parted the batwings and stepped inside The Buffalo. Mayor Whittaker, dressed like an undertaker in a black derby hat and matching suit and tie, stood hands clasped alongside half a dozen of the Town Committee. Their faces all beamed their gratitude. Wolf and Dale Procter had the town in their grip. No one was safe. Shop owners had to pay them ten per cent 'protection' money. They prodded and bullied the town citizens. Someone had suggested they raise a town posse to rid their community of these vermin. It was generally accepted it was a great idea, but no one put up his hand to join.

'Would you like a drink, on the house?'

'Thank God you came, Mr Cassidy.'

'You were highly recommended.'

'We heard you cleaned up Hellhole.'

Brett ignored the questions and compliments. He'd heard most of them before in other towns. He wanted to get down to the business in hand and then ride on, because he meant this to be the last time he hired out his guns. He'd survived many gunfights, killed many hellions who deserved to die, and he was still around to tell the tale. The way Brett Cassidy saw it, there comes a time when a man who's lived by the gun needs to put it away and change his ways, maybe even settle down.

That time had come.

This was his last mission.

'Where are they?' Brett demanded.

'When they're not raising hell, they're

usually drinking whiskey in an old woodsman's cabin by Turner's Mill,' Reilly the local newspaperman said. He was the newest member of the Jericho Creek Town Committee, elected on his thirtieth birthday last year. One day, folks said, he would aspire to be Mayor Reilly. For now he was owner-editor of the *Jericho Creek Herald*. Addressing Brett, he said, 'I saw both Wolf and Dale lounging outside the cabin an hour ago. Wolf looks exactly like his name, lean and hungry, always dresses in black. Dale's not like his brother. He's a real dandy, fancies himself as a ladies' man, but don't be fooled, Mr Cassidy, he's the fastest of the two.'

Brett turned and looked over the bat-wings. 'Where's Turner's Mill?'

'Down Main Street just past the emigrant wagons,' Mayor Whittaker supplied helpfully. 'Ebenezer Turner, being a good neighbourly Mennonite, allows his couple of town acres there to be used as a jumping off place for homesteaders heading west across the Plains. Reckon there are half a dozen prairie schooners and some livestock waiting there for the word to roll the wagons, which should be tomorrow morning.'

Brett looked down on Main Street, his eyes slowly scanning its length until they found the white canvas of emigrant wagons. West of the wagons, just down the street, was Turner's Mill, a plain wooden building standing on the banks of a swiftly running creek. The mill's big wheel was slowly churning water into white foam. Right beside the mill was an old log cabin with a single, curtained window.

'Do the Procters have any sidekicks I need to watch out for?' Brett asked.

'Well, there's Miller,' the newspaper-man said. 'He plays poker with Wolf.'

'Miller's of no account, gutless,' Whittaker dismissed the slick tinhorn. 'He'll be hiding under a poker table once the shooting starts.'

'What about Dunn?' the bartender put in.

'Abe Dunn, town bully,' Reilly

informed Brett. 'He's been swaggering up and down Main Street like a prize turkey ever since the Procters arrived. He might as well be one of them. In fact, some say he has joined them.'

'You can't miss Dunn,' the bartender said, sliding a bottle of rye whiskey to a red-eyed cowpoke who looked like he'd had more than enough, even at this relatively early hour. 'Bald as a hen's egg, never wears a hat. Gun slung low on his left side.'

Brett waited but no one else spoke.

He turned and said simply, 'Time to earn my keep.'

He parted the batwings and stepped outside.

Dark clouds edged across the face of the dying sun as he walked down the slight slope, headed by two empty cattle yards as he reached Main Street. He passed a couple of old timers asleep on their boardwalk rockers and heard the rasp of keys locking doors. Two nervous women hurried home. A mongrel dog yapped incessantly as Brett strode by the town's general store. The store-keeper grabbed his dog and hauled it inside. Brett kept to the western board-walk and crossed the alley between the stone-walled Mennonite church and the sombre, black-fronted undertaker's par-lour that had two coffins displayed out front. Just past the mortician's shop, Rosie McPhee hastily closed and locked her tea room door. Still walking, Brett reached the wagons standing haphaz-ardly on Turner's acres. With his eyes fixed on the cabin beside the mill, Brett only afforded the homesteaders a quick glance. Mostly they were tending their animals, although three of the women stood around a cooking fire. He smelled buffalo steaks heating in the embers. One tall raven-haired man and his attractive wife stood close to the street watching as he strode past them.

Brett was just one hundred paces away from the mill.

On the left side of the street, the bespectacled little telegraph office oper-ator pulled down his window shades.

11

There was a man lingering in his office doorway. He didn't have a hair on his scarred scalp and his single, pearl-handled gun was slung low against his left thigh.

'Dunn?' Brett demanded, halting.

'What's it to you?' came the insolent response.

'Walk ahead of me.'

Dunn smirked. 'Like hell!'

Brett's next words cut like a knife. 'You have a choice, Dunn. Do like I say or I'll put a slug in both of your legs and you'll be walking on crutches for a long time.'

The town bully hesitated. Blood pulsed in bulging blue rivers along his temple. He didn't like being pushed around, especially as he knew some of the townsfolk were watching, but there was something about this tall man with the cold eyes and twin Colts that unnerved him. Pin pricks of sweat sprang to his bald head.

Dunn shrugged. 'OK, Mister, have it your way. Let's walk.'

The bully took twenty steps before

Brett said, 'That's far enough.' Dunn stayed where he was, boots planted in the dust as the gunfighter gave his next order, 'Call your friends from their snake hole.'

Dunn hesitated, sweat now trickling over his baldness.

'Now!'

Despite his fears, Dunn still tried to put on a brave face in front of any towners who were watching or listening. He quipped, 'If you say so, boss.'

'Quit the smart talk. Just do it.'

Shrugging, Dunn cupped his mouth with his hands and bellowed, 'Wolf! Dale! You have a visitor.'

The cabin door creaked slowly open. At first Brett saw a mere shadow, then Wolf Procter stood framed there. He was just as Reilly had described. Lean, all skin and bone, cadaverous-looking, dressed in grimy black shirt, pants and shiny polished boots. Predatory eyes became twin slits as Wolf Procter appraised the man he knew had been summoned to kill him.

When Wolf spoke, his words were deceptively soft.

'Heard about you, Cassidy.'

Brett looked past him, but he could see no one else in the room. Of course, Dale could be concealed there.

'Where's your dandy brother?'

'Mindin' his own flamin' business like you should be — that's if you know what's good for you, which I doubt,' Wolf said, still quietly.

'Call him,' Brett demanded.

Wolf Procter merely stared at him, smirking confidently. He had a shiny silver sawn-off shotgun resting in his right holster. If he managed to aim it and pull the trigger, it would unleash a lethal storm of flying lead.

'Go to hell,' Wolf challenged.

Suddenly a hoarse warning rang out from the wagon camp.

'Behind you! Tea house roof!'

Instinctively, Brett Cassidy threw himself sideways, clearing leather as he crunched against the side of the board-walk. Two rifle bullets blasted into the dust, right where he'd been standing a split second earlier. Wedged against the boardwalk, Brett looked up at the tea house roof. He fired a single shot from his right side gun and Dale Procter, staked out alongside the tin chimney on the iron roof, stopped the bullet square in his chest. The rifle slid from the dandy's grasp, bounced down over the roof and spun into the side alley. Rosie McPhee screamed at her window as the dandy crashed headlong past her and sprawled over the tea house's boardwalk.

Crouching, Brett saw Wolf lift his double-barrelled shotgun from its leather holster, but the killer didn't even get to aim his weapon because the gunfighter's twin Colts thundered in deadly unison. Two bullets blasted Wolf Procter clean off his feet and blew him back through the cabin door. He crashed against a cupboard and dropped lifelessly to the earth floor.

Brett reared to his feet as Dunn backed to the wooden front of Turner's Mill. He hadn't come for Dunn but he figured he might as well rid Jericho Creek of this bully too — or at least render him harmless. Deciding on the latter, he levelled both guns at him. With both Procters dead, Dunn was friendless. Ashen-faced, whimpering like a whipped dog, Dunn pleaded for his life but when Brett ordered him to drop his gun, he still kept clutching the weapon. Not wanting to take any chances, Brett shot a bullet into each of his legs and he crumbled into the dust. Brett booted the gun from Dunn's grasp.

'Reckon your bully-boy days are over, *hombre*,' Brett told the squirming man. 'I'll leave you for the doc's knife, then the carpenter's crutches.'

He sheathed his guns.

Twelve killings, an even dozen and another liberated town.

But, as he'd told himself when he rode in, it was time to pack away those guns. There was just one thing he needed to do before he rode out.

He walked back up the street to where the wagons waited for their trek west across the Plains. The homesteaders were making ready now. Tomorrow they would set out from Jericho Creek, on the last part of their great adventure. The tall, dark-haired man and his slim young wife had mugs of coffee in their hands as they stood by a cooking fire.

'Figured it was you who shouted the warning,' Brett said.

'Yes, it was my husband,' the woman said proudly.

'Tom McBeath,' the settler introduced himself. 'And from what we heard in the town this past week, you're Mr Cassidy.'

'That's me,' Brett confirmed to the two homesteaders.

'Nice shooting,' McBeath complimented him.

Brett made no comment.

'We're on our way west, Mr Cassidy,' Tom McBeath said. Willowy, he was in his thirties, clean-shaven, deep brown eyes and a prominent nose. He wore no guns, but there was a knife sheathed at his belt. 'Heading for Lonesome Valley to stake our claim for those hundred and sixty acres the Government says we can farm. Praise the Lord for the Homesteader Act.'

These were good people, Brett thought, the very salt of the earth. They were the new breed of folks who would settle the Western frontier, the future backbone of the nation. He wished them well. Although he couldn't change his past or what he had become, in this moment he envied them for their lives.

'I'm here to thank you,' Brett said simply.

Tom acknowledged Brett's gratitude with a nod. 'We've been in Jericho Creek for two weeks now, waiting to join the main wagon train when it finally arrives,' he explained. 'We've heard about and seen what the Procters have done to this town. My wife, Harmony, witnessed the one they call Wolf paw a decent woman in the general store and then kill a man who tried to help her. I don't often use foul language, Mr Cassidy, but I'll say it now — and may the Lord forgive me for this profanity — the Procters were

18

bastards.'

'Tom!' Mrs McBeath gasped at his outburst.

But Tom McBeath would not be restrained. 'And when I saw one of the bastards on the roof ready to shoot you in the back, I knew what I had to do.'

'You saved my life, Tom McBeath, and I owe you,' Brett told him.

'I did what was right.'

Brett afforded them both one of his rare smiles and said, 'Have a safe journey west and have a happy life. So long, my friends.'

He turned away from them and strode back up Main Street where doors were being unlocked and curtains drawn open. He saw the town doctor with his black bag and bottle of whiskey waddle from an alley, making his way to where Dunn was writhing in pain alone on the street. The undertaker's doors creaked open and the mortician rubbed his hands as he contemplated fresh business. The Town Committee would pay him to arrange two paupers' burials. He wouldn't earn much but it would help pay the loan on his shop. A few folks thanked Brett Cassidy as he made his way to the saloon. Once inside, some of the eager patrons offered to buy him drinks but one was enough for him.

'Where you headed for?' Mayor Whittaker asked conversationally.

'I'll start with Brown Bear Pass, then maybe winter in Buckskin.'

'When you get to Buckskin, look up John and Grace Walters, old friends of mine,' the mayor suggested, 'They run the post office there.' He added, 'Grace makes the best blueberry pies I've ever tasted.'

Brett promised, 'I'll call on them for sure.'

'Once again, Mr Cassidy, on behalf of the citizens of Jericho Creek, I thank you for what you've done for this town,' Mayor Whittaker began a speech.

But Brett didn't need a speech. He simply wished Mayor Whittaker and his committee men well, walked outside the saloon and remounted his roan.

Dusk closed over Jericho Creek as Brett Cassidy rode Main Street for the last time. He slowed his roan as he drew adjacent to the wagons. There were more homesteaders standing around cooking fires now, but he managed to distinguish the McBeaths. Tom was conversing earnestly with another pioneer, an older man wearing a Confederate cap with a long, straggly white beard flowing down over his old army tunic.

Harmony McBeath was stirring soup with a long wooden spoon.

Just as Brett rode by, she happened to look up.

Harmony's eyes followed the gunfighter's shadowy figure and in turn Brett saw her plainly because the firelight danced on her long honey-coloured hair and pretty face. She was truly a beautiful woman and Tom McBeath was a lucky man. Harmony stopped stirring the soup and he caught her fleeting smile.

Moments later Brett Cassidy was gone, swallowed by the deepening dusk.

He rode right out of town.

The distant starlit peaks beckoned him north.

* * *

That night Brett made camp in a sheltered hollow on the southern bank of the Red Stone River. He lit a small cooking fire, rubbed down his horse, then picked up his rifle. He made a lean shadow in the moonlight as he retraced his roan's hoof marks to the edge of the forest he'd just ridden through. There he backed between two trees and waited in the darkness. He'd learned a lesson very soon after becoming a gunfighter. Hired by the Wichita Wells Town Committee, he'd earned a thousand dollars by gunning down triple-murderer Abe Harrison. With the cash in his saddle bag, he'd ridden out of town and lit a camp fire, just like he'd done tonight. Right on sundown, shadowy riders came out of the dusk. They were Harrison's brother and two friends, bent on

22

revenge and collecting Brett's payment. In the ensuing gunfight, Judah Harrison, shot in the chest, crashed from his horse. Seeing Harrison dead in the cold dust, the sidekicks fled, but not before one of them turned in his saddle and emptied his gun. The last bullet ripped into Brett's left thigh.

Now, staked out in these trees, Brett recalled that night, how he'd bandaged his wound and made it to the doctor's surgery in the next town. From that time on, he'd always checked his back-trail. If a man carried a lot of money, he could well be a target. And so tonight he waited, telling himself that this should be the last time he needed to do this. Very soon he would be in the mountains and he would no longer be Brett Cassidy, professional gunfighter, but just another westerner.

And he would have no regrets.

He waited till midnight, waited till the fire he'd lit burned low so all he could see were small flames licking a blackened log. He heard nothing except the hoot of an owl and the sound made by a snake slithering through pine needles. There was no pursuit. The Procters had no secret friends, neither were any Jericho Creek layabouts foolish enough to pursue him. Brett was relieved, not because he was afraid of a gunfight, but because he'd had enough of killing.

Finally, he emerged from the pines and walked back to his camp.

There, in the early hours of the morning, with the watery moon high in the starlit sky, he roasted a deer steak and heated his coffee pot in the glowing coals.

For the first time in over a decade, Brett Cassidy felt free.

* * *

Brett Cassidy was in no hurry so he took his time.

Leaving behind his first night camp out of Jericho Creek, he forded the shallow Red Stone River and climbed the twisting mountain trails. Eagles flew overhead and he saw the white, furtive eyes of wolves in the darkness when he made night camps. He sheltered in a shallow cave when a wild storm drenched the mountains and made the peaks glisten with early snow. It was a lonely, silent world, but he felt at home already.

His Colt Peacemakers no longer sat in twin holsters.

They were packed away in his saddle-bag.

His only visible weapon was a long rifle resting in its saddle scabbard. It was his hunting rifle and he used it once to kill a stag for food.

He saw few people as he rode north. One cloudy morning he came across a couple of whiskery prospectors too busy to talk, intent instead on panning for elusive gold nuggets in a creek. Three days further into the mountains he met a lone hunter resting his horse in a forest clearing. The hunter gave him the name 'Jones' which Brett accepted without comment. He'd met quite a few men named 'Smith' or 'Jones' on this lonely frontier. Some, he'd learned later, were actually on the run. Nevertheless, he shared his camp fire coffee and a couple of cigarettes with him. One stormy late afternoon, a week later, an old timer leading two burros crossed his trail. He thought the old coot was crazy, gabbling on non-stop while knocking back a jug full of red-eye whiskey. Brett was glad to see the ancient mountain man move out next morning.

He was the last living soul he saw for a month.

Not that this mattered to Brett Cassidy.

He didn't mind being alone. Maybe he needed to be right now.

Winter approaching, he set his face for the mining camp that hugged the creek in Brown Bear Pass. Brett knew that Big Sam Bush, an old friend from his army days, ran a trading post there that stocked everything from flour to frontier newspapers. He also had the agency for the Hudson Bay Trading Company.

Brett looped his reins around the tie-rail and strolled into the trading post.

'Doggone it! Trooper Cassidy!'

'Howdy, Sam.'

'Haven't set eyes on you since we were both discharged from Fort Glory!' Sam Bush exclaimed. He came around the counter and the two men shook hands. 'But I've heard all about you, Brett. Yes, sir, I certainly have. You're a legend all over the frontier.' He thrust his pipe between his lips and asked in a serious tone, 'Hey, where are those guns I've heard stories about?'

'I'll explain over a beer.'

'Or two or three,' Sam Bush raised his shaggy eyebrows, then roared with laughter. 'I remember the time in the barracks when we both knocked back half a dozen and were still fit for duty.'

'Long time ago, Sam,' Brett reminded him.

'Yeah, we were both kids, wet behind the ears.'

They yarned long into the night, mostly about their exploits at Fort Glory, while Big Sam's petite Arapaho woman, whom he called Nina, knitted a shawl by the glowing coals in the fireplace. She was half his age and half his size and her name meant 'Singer'. Sam explained that drunken white prospectors had murdered her man in a midnight brawl and he'd found her wandering distraught and vulnerable in a wooded valley just beyond Brown Bear Pass. He'd brought her home to his trading post and she'd chosen to stay, proud now to be known as Big Sam's woman.

'Hanging up your guns was smart,' Big Sam complimented him, downing his last beer. 'You'll live longer.'

'That's what I figure.'

Seeing his Arapaho woman in the doorway beckoning him, Big Sam hauled himself out of his rocker chair and said, 'Now you must excuse me. My woman wants me and I know what for!'

'Go to it, Sam.'

'Uh, Nina has a kid sister who can be pretty accommodating,' Sam mentioned. 'If you stay for a couple of nights I can arrange for her to be here for you.' He grinned. 'You won't regret it. She can be mighty friendly to a man like you.'

Brett stayed two nights in a room out at the back of Big Sam's Trading Post, but he politely declined his old friend's offer. He'd never had a woman arranged for him. He always chose his own. Early on the third day Brett bought some supplies and saddled his horse.

'I'm heading north,' Brett told him.

'You're welcome to stay if you like,' his old army friend invited.

'Thanks for the offer but I aim to winter in Buckskin.'

'That's a nice quiet town,' Big Sam said.

'My kinda place.' Brett remarked.

'Drop in anytime,' Big Sam invited.

Brett rode out of the mining camp and took the river trail that probed higher into the mountains. Clouds were gathering, billowing and laden with snow.

Winter would come early this year.

2

It was late in the Summer of '69.

Brett Cassidy was riding a well-worn forest trail after checking his traps. This was his weekly ritual and took most of the day as he normally set his traps down-river, past the falls, well out of town in the deep shadow of Tomahawk Mountain.

Today he was returning with over a dozen beavers. Their pelts, when dried out, would join over fifty others hanging in his cabin. When they were all ready, he'd pack them in bags and pay Big Sam's trading post one of his regular visits. There he'd spend time with his old army friend and the now very-pregnant Nina. Sam and the Arapaho woman had been pronounced man and wife by a visiting Methodist preacher who'd agreed to conduct the ceremony as long as there was no liquor in sight. Brett had attended the wedding and sold some pelts at the same time.

Agency prices varied month by month, but mostly his pelts made him enough money to pay his bills and live comfortably in his single-roomed log cabin, just on the verge of the mountain town of Buckskin.

Mind you, Brett sometimes thought, his income had taken a huge dive since leaving his gun-fighting days behind him and putting away his twin Colts, but not once had he regretted his decision.

He was quite content being Brett Cassidy, trapper.

It was close to sundown as he forded the river that flowed by Buckskin and joined the track that threaded through tall pines to three trappers' cabins. His was the last one in the row, built with his own hands when he first arrived and decided to make a new life in Buckskin almost five years ago.

He headed past the first cabin. Trapper Ben raised his hand in greeting. He was thin as a rake, heavily bearded, son of German emigrants. He'd been here as long as folks could remember. The second cabin belonged to Abraham. That was the name the wiry little man answered to and he'd never given a surname to anyone. Folks said confidentially to each other that he was once an outlaw specialising in stagecoach hold-ups, but he minded his own business so no one asked questions. Brett's place was just down from Abraham's. Once home, he would light his woodstove, cook a quick meal, brew some coffee and have an early night. Sometimes he'd play cards with Ben or ride down and have a drink in Buckskin's quiet, often half-empty saloon, The Lucky Deuce, but tonight he'd stay home.

Closing in on his cabin, Brett saw he had visitors.

Buckskin's postmaster, lanky, short-sighted John Walters, and his comely grey-haired wife, Grace, were waiting for him.

He had a letter in his left hand and she had a blueberry pie in her right one.

'Good evening, Brett,' John Walters

greeted. He peered through his horn-rimmed spectacles. 'I see you have a full bag.'

'Now I just have to skin them,' Brett responded as he rode in and halted his snorting horse. He grinned as he emptied his saddle. 'So what's this? A welcome-home committee or are you still trying to persuade me to sing in your Sunday morning church choir?'

'Not this time. It's just a friendly visit,' John assured him.

'Reverend Pendleton reckons we're wasting our breath trying to persuade a sinner like you to come to church,' Grace said good-naturedly.

'The preacher's right,' Brett agreed. 'Mind you, if I could find myself a willing woman, he can marry us in his church.'

'Well, there is Avis White,' the post-master suggested, grinning.

Brett raised his eyebrows at the mention of the town's most formidable spinster. Miss Avis White kept her six-roomed home so spotlessly clean that men were too scared to enter lest they soil her carpets. Besides that, saloon talk said she was so pure in heart that no man could get even close to her.

'Forget Avis,' Brett said.

'Figured you'd say that,' Walters said.

'So what have I done to earn this friendly visit?' Brett asked.

John Walters explained, 'We're here for two reasons, Brett. First, a letter arrived for you. Actually, the person who sent it obviously didn't know where you live because it's addressed to Mr Brett Cassidy, care of Mayor Whittaker, Jericho Creek, with a note written right across the front saying 'please forward on if you know where Mr Cassidy resides'. Fortunately, Mayor Whittaker must have recalled you said you were headed this way. He took a chance and forwarded it to Buckskin post office. Figured it might be important so Grace and me decided to deliver it in person on our evening walk.'

He handed the letter to Brett.

It was a brown crinkled envelope with a small tear across the top and the two stamps peeling off the paper, testimony to the fact it had been roughly manhandled on its journey. He turned the letter over. The sender's name was in capital letters.

MRS H. McBEATH.

Instantly Brett recalled her, particularly that last smile as she'd looked up from the cooking fire while he rode past on his way out of Jericho Creek. And he remembered her husband especially, Tom McBeath, the homesteader whose timely shout had saved his life.

'And here's the second reason for our visit — a homemade blueberry pie,' Grace Walters said.

Blueberry pies made by the postmaster's wife had almost legendary status in Buckskin and she was most generous handing them out to men who had no wives to cook for them.

Brett said gratefully, 'I'm obliged to both of you. Will you stay for coffee?'

'Thanks for the offer, but we'll leave you to your letter reading and pie,' the postmaster spoke for them both.

Brett thanked them again and went inside where he lit his oil lamp and cut the letter open with the sharp point of his hunting knife. There in the flickering yellow light, he read the smudged, hand-written words. He read them twice, the second time very slowly. Then he folded the letter before going outside to tend his horse while his wood-stove heated his coffee pot and warmed Grace's blueberry pie.

When he returned inside, he first drank the hot coffee.

And his eyes strayed to the black metal box just visible under his bunk.

It was where he kept his two Colt Peacemaker guns.

An owl hooted ominously outside in the darkness.

* * *

Brett Cassidy saw the smoke just before noon.

It rose in small dark puffs from a long, sweeping ridge and floated slowly into the azure sky.

Watching the smoke, he drew his roan into the shadows of a lone pine. He was now three weeks out of Jericho Creek where he'd first latched onto this westward trail. He was well aware he was on the edge of Cheyenne Territory and although he was riding along a wheel-rutted trail used by Wells Fargo stagecoaches and westbound wagon trains, he knew he wasn't actually in Indian country.

Nevertheless, Brett was wary.

He wouldn't be taking any chances.

As far as he knew, there was relative peace between the white settlers and the Cheyenne Indians, but it would pay to be cautious, especially as in an hour's time this trail would drop through two narrow passes, both perfect for an ambush. Hopefully, however, that wasn't on their minds. He just kept riding.

Deciding to rest his horse, still the same one he'd ridden for the last seven years, Brett dismounted and took a swig from his water canteen. He saw more smoke, this time rising from a bald rim the other side of the trail.

He'd once wintered in a Cheyenne village, a welcome guest after he'd rescued one of their maidens from the unwelcome advances of two drunken traders who'd made up their minds to take advantage of her. A bullet in one man's foot and a second slug shattering the other's left forearm sent them on their way muttering threats they would never carry out. At the time, the Cheyenne elders, very impressed, wanted to marry him off to the young maiden concerned, but Brett had politely but firmly declined. They weren't impressed by his decision, but they still let him stay as the snows set in. It was there Brett Cassidy learned the Cheyenne lingo. Not that it was any help right now. Cheyenne tribes were scattered for hundreds of miles across the Plains. He was a month's ride from the village he'd wintered in. Any Cheyenne riders in these parts wouldn't know him and, if they had a killing on their minds, he'd be fair game.

So Brett kept his rifle handy while resting the roan.

He had his six-shooters nestling in their holsters too. They hadn't been sheathed there for a long time and their weight against his thighs brought back memories he thought he'd put behind him.

Harmony McBeath's letter was in his shirt pocket. It was brief and poignant, obviously written out of sheer desperation, the words smudged by tear stains.

We are in terrible trouble, Mr Cassidy.
Our lives are in danger.
We need help.
Would you consider coming out of retirement?
I don't know who else to turn to.
Harmony McBeath, Lonesome Valley

It was signed and dated three months ago with a grim postscript across the bottom of her note:

Sadly, my husband Tom passed away.

Brett Cassidy, living the peaceful life of a mountain trapper, had kept to his resolute decision not to strap on his gunfighter's Colts again. He'd been enjoying life in Buckskin. The townsfolk had accepted him. He was making a living out of pelts and the sound of gunshots and smell of sudden death seemed far, far away.

But Harmony's letter had changed all that.

If the request had come from anyone else, he'd have probably ignored it, but he couldn't forget the day Tom McBeath saved his life and what he'd said after the gunfight: '*I owe you.*'

Maybe it was a long time ago, but those words amounted to a promise. He certainly owed Tom and, now he was dead, he owed his widow.

Harmony's note was short on detail. He had no idea what 'terrible trouble' she was referring to and how many were affected. Before leaving Buckskin, he'd asked around. Hardly anyone had heard of Lonesome Valley, let alone any trouble there. It was purely a destination for homesteaders on wagon trains. He'd called on Big Sam on the way south and had a couple of drinks while the trader rummaged through a pile of newspapers.

'If there's been a ruckus in Lonesome Valley, it's sure been hushed up,' Big Sam said, shaking his head because the only reference to that valley he found was about some Cheyennes burning an abandoned cabin there. It was hardly a headline story and the reporter offered no reason for the arson. 'Probably did it for the hell of it,' Sam shrugged.

Brett remounted his roan.

He headed west again, keeping in the saddle until the shadows stretched across the trail. He rode through the pass without incident, not seeing any Indians. Of course, they could well be there, concealed, silent watchers. In addition, he hadn't seen any more Cheyenne smoke signals, but he decided not to light a cooking fire. Instead he ate beef and biscuits he'd packed in his saddle-bag.

He didn't sleep. He merely used the

night to rest his horse, and one hour before first light he was on the trail again. Early in the day a Wells Fargo stagecoach came swaying out of a cloud of billowing dust. The driver was in no mood to spend the time of day with a lone traveller like Brett Cassidy and his eastbound stage thundered past him. The man riding shotgun merely waved.

An hour later Brett came upon Mesa way station, stopping briefly to water his horse in the slow-moving creek behind the dusty log building. There was but one man there, the morose owner, Bart Bayer, who lived there alone. He sold essential supplies, ammunition and had reward dodgers pinned to his walls. If any stage travellers stopping over wanted beds for the night, there were five old bunks for which he charged a dollar each a night, pillow and blanket extra.

Bayer wasn't exactly talkative, but when Brett bought a beer, he did offer a warning, 'Watch out for Cheyennes.'

'Seen their smoke and they've been

shadowing me.'

Bayer shrugged his bony shoulders. 'Varmints haven't given trouble for years, but for some reason they're uncommonly restless right now. Keep your guns handy.'

Brett thanked him and rode out.

It was then, one mile west of the way station, that Brett saw two Indian riders following him along the sandstone rim that overlooked the stage trail. They were out of range, but Brett didn't intend to use his rifle unless he had to. They had a right to ride that rim same as he had the right to this trail. He'd just keep an eye on them.

They followed him at a distance as he crossed a sagebrush flat and then headed down the dusty stage road into a steep-walled pass littered with towering arrowhead pines and a hundred marbled boulders. Ancient caves were like hollow eyes peering down at him. A couple of buzzards circled.

From what he'd been told, this was Sundown Pass.

Soon it would empty into his destination, Lonesome Valley.

And the Cheyennes were still shadowing him.

They were closer now, close enough for Brett to see that one was an older Indian, his face wrinkled and brown, thin, his shirt and pants made of skins. His companion was much younger, red-faced, long raven-black hair.

Brett could easily lift his rifle and take one, maybe both, but there was no real reason. He might have spent many years gun-fighting, but when he killed it was because he had to. However, now he kept his right hand resting on his rifle stock. Wary, he rode right through the pass to the flat rim that made a windswept balcony over a long, deep basin.

Lonesome Valley stretched below him.

He saw valley walls that were old and crumbling, eaten away by countless centuries of blazing sun, high winds and winter blizzards. He glimpsed a thin track hugging the rims on the valley's northern side. Fed by a slow-flowing river,

Lonesome Valley's grasses were greener than he'd seen thus far on his westward ride. It was a verdant, sheltered valley, dotted with trees, perfect for settlement.

Sitting saddle on this high rim, Brett Cassidy saw where the trail dropped from the pass to cut a swathe through a dozen homesteaders' acres. These landholdings looked like pieces of a patchwork quilt all the way to a distant town.

Brett nudged his roan into a steady walk and headed down-trail.

The two Cheyennes were still following him, riding together but keeping their distance.

He passed by the first acreage.

The Homesteader Act permitted settlers to settle on one hundred and sixty acres of public land. If the settlers remained there for five continuous years, they received official ownership. Brett had heard of homesteaders who'd found it almost impossible to get a living out of their holdings because of adverse soil conditions or lack of water, but Lonesome Valley looked to be good arable land and, by the time he'd ridden by the fourth homesteader spread, he'd seen plentiful cattle and sheep grazing and abundant crops growing.

He had no idea which part of the valley the McBeaths had staked out so he just kept riding, checking each spread as he passed by. Some pieces of land had signs nailed to their gate posts. Some just bore names, like 'Kincaid', 'Jefferson' and 'Will Quade'. Others were more pretentious like 'Lex's Range', 'Buck's Place' and 'Rankin's Homestead'. Brett had just passed Will Quade's spread when he came across a small, splintery wooden sign overhanging a wire gate.

The word 'McBeath', originally painted in large red lettering, had been faded by the sun. Under 'McBeath' were the words 'Tom and Harmony's Place'.

Brett reined his horse and looked back over his shoulder.

The Cheyennes too had halted their pinto ponies. The younger one raised his rifle and brandished it high above his head. It looked to be a deliberate act of defiance and provocation and Brett's fingers closed over his rifle stock. But those fingers stayed there. He recalled the way station owner's warning about the Cheyennes being restless and he wasn't here to fire the first shot possibly leading to an Indian War. He heard the old Cheyenne warrior speak sharply to the younger, impetuous brave. At first the young buck spoke back, arguing, belittling the older man, but finally he reluctantly agreed to lower his rifle.

Moments later, both Indian riders turned their ponies and retreated to a wooded hollow. Brett saw the movement of pine branches, then he glimpsed the Cheyennes heading back towards the pass.

Brett waited, watching them for a full minute before opening the gate and riding through. The McBeath land was undulating, sandwiched between Quade's place and another property that at a quick glance looked to have been abandoned. Harmony's grass rolled down to a distant willow-lined creek which made a natural boundary, separating it from yet another homesteader spread.

The one hundred and sixty acres were fully enclosed by a fence that Brett could see needed mending in places. Riding down a straight, narrow track, he saw sheep, a couple of goats and a milking cow. He came across a wagon with torn canvas, obviously the one that had carried their belongings west. Past the wagon, and fenced separately, was an acre of corn. He rode by rows of beans, potatoes and pumpkins.

Ahead he saw a cabin constructed with hewn logs cemented together by dried mud. It was a small dwelling, not even as large as the one he'd raised for himself after retiring in Buckskin. He saw a single window with green curtains drawn right across, the door shut. A thin wisp of smoke rose from a tin chimney in the slate roof. The cabin seemed wreathed in silence. Not even a dog barked.

He slowed his roan to a walk.

That's when he heard the whine of a door's hinges.

The cabin door inched open just wide enough for him to see the naked muzzle of a rifle protruding. Then he glimpsed a furtive eye framed just above the rifle.

He called to her, 'Mrs McBeath.'

The door was slowly pushed open until Harmony McBeath stood there.

Then her eyes lit up as she recognised him.

Trembling, she gasped and leaned her rifle against the door frame.

'Mr Cassidy! It's you!' she cried incredulously. 'Thank God you've come!'

3

Harmony watched the tall man dismount in the shadow of her cabin.

She was thinking he hadn't changed much since that afternoon when she'd first seen and admired him in Jericho Creek. He was still lean, an imposing figure of a man, not an ounce of fat on his strong, muscular body. His hair, straight, needing a cut and poking out beneath his Stetson, was still black like a raven, not even a hint of greyness. And she remembered those eyes. They were still eyes that drew you, eyes of gratitude and friendship, with a hint of coldness. But now however, those eyes were smiling.

'Good to see you, Mrs McBeath,' Brett Cassidy said, tethering the roan to a hitching post by her lean-to stable. He looked straight at her as he added sincerely, 'Sorry to hear about Mr McBeath.'

'Tom was a good man,' Harmony said as he finished securing the roan. 'He's been gone for over two years now, buried in the cemetery just outside the town of Red Butte, that's down-valley from here. There's a section reserved for we homesteaders, fenced off from the rest of the cemetery.' She lamented, 'And there are quite a few graves there already.' Her soft blue eyes found and held his. 'Far too many, Mr Cassidy.'

Brett walked to her. He was so tall that the top of Harmony's head just reached the ridge of his broad shoulders. 'May I ask how it happened? Frontier fever?'

Harmony replied, 'Horse riding accident. Leastways, that's what the Red Butte coroner said in his report.' She faltered and said, 'Guess I should scratch Tom's name off the sign on the gate. I just haven't felt like doing it. I mean, taking his name off seems so final, doesn't it?'

'My condolences, ma'am,' Brett said, feeling that any words he would say at this time would be inadequate.

Harmony changed the subject, inviting, 'You've ridden a long way so please come inside, Mr Cassidy. It's a small, humble home Tom and I built with our own hands. Took us three weeks and it rained most of the time. No one helped us.' She reiterated, 'Come in and make yourself at home. I brew good coffee and it so happens there's a cake baking in the oven.'

'Thank you, ma'am.'

Brett followed her inside. It was indeed small and humble, but it was homely. It had a woman's touch with a decorative picture quilt affixed to the wall. A potbelly stove warmed the single room which was sparsely furnished with a table, two chairs, wardrobe and pantry. A hanging curtain half concealed a double bed bunk and dressing table.

'I wasn't sure whether you'd come,' Harmony said. 'After all, I had heard from several folks that you were no longer a professional gunfighter.'

'I had put away my guns, Mrs McBeath,' he said.

'But you're wearing them now,' Harmony observed.

'Yes, ma'am,' Brett affirmed quietly.

She poured strong, aromatic coffee for them both and took the freshly-baked johnnycake out of the oven. It smelled good.

'By the date on your letter, it took almost two months to reach me,' Brett explained as she cut the cake. Her hands, he noticed, were hardened from manual work. With her husband under the clay, she'd had to do everything herself. He said, 'I came as soon as I received it.'

'For which I'm very grateful,' she told him.

'Your letter said there was big trouble in Lonesome Valley,' Brett prompted.

'Yes, very big trouble.'

'I'm here to listen so tell me about it, Mrs McBeath.'

'Please call me Harmony,' she requested.

He thought about that. 'Be a pleasure, Harmony.'

He watched her sip her coffee. She

had full lips and beautiful white teeth. In fact, he told himself, she was a fine-looking woman all over. Her full breasts and slim hips filled out her long gingham dress to perfection and her long hair made a rich golden cascade that kissed her slim shoulders.

'At first when we arrived in Lonesome Valley, we thought it was Paradise,' Harmony remembered. 'Sheltered, lots of pasture, good soil for growing crops, friendly Indians and folks in Red Butte welcomed us. The town preacher, Mr O'Toole, even arranged a special service for us and the church folk put on morning coffee. We staked out our land, all legally, built our homes, bought goods from town traders, then began to fence our individual acreages off. Things were fine until a slimy snake named Garth Delaney began prodding us. Have you ever heard of this snake Delaney?'

Brett frowned at the mention of this name. He'd never actually met anyone called Delaney, but he remembered an old-time saloon friend, Buzzard Crocker, who could out-drink any man and play poker like a tinhorn gambler, once named his 'three most ornery skunks in the west'. One was a back-shooting renegade named Sanderson, the second was Colorado's rogue lawman, Baines. The third, he proclaimed, was a certain Garth Delaney, card cheat, wife-stealer, killer and someone who should have had a noose tightened around his neck years ago. According to Buzzard, Delaney was a 'low-down rat' who snuck out of Kansas when 'things became too goddamn hot for him'.

'I've heard of him,' Brett said simply.

Harmony continued, 'Delaney arrived here just a few months after we came. He bought the Lazy F Ranch, that's the spread shaped like a diamond just this side of Red Butte. He also took over the Last Chance Saloon and then the general store. Most of the homesteaders don't spend time in saloons so that didn't matter, but he doubled prices on flour, salt, seeds, utensils, fencing wire and suchlike in the store, meaning some of us couldn't afford most of the essentials we need.'

'Sounds like a real low-down rat,' Brett quoted Buzzard Crocker.

'There's more, Mr Cassidy.'

'If I'm to call you Harmony, then I'm Brett.'

She hesitated at this, but then said finally, 'Brett, there's more. Garth Delaney's greedy. He has a perfectly good spread of land, acres of good grass, well watered, but that's not enough for him. He's made it quite plain he wants to double his herd, but to do that he'd have to use more grass than he owns and graze his cattle on public land.'

'And you homesteaders have fenced off the only available public land in Lonesome Valley,' Brett stated.

'Precisely, Brett.'

'So Garth Delaney's been prodding you,' he guessed.

'At first there was some fence cutting in the night, stacks of hay mysteriously set alight, couple of gates opened so stock strayed and sheep stolen,' Harmony said bitterly. 'Then Delaney began turning the townsfolk against us, even the medico and the sheriff. Some townsfolk are employed by him so they do like he says. He cut out all credit for homesteaders at his general store so now we not only have to pay his inflated prices but we also have to pay cash.' She paused, breasts heaving. Speaking more softly now, she asked, 'Hope the cake's tasty enough for you?'

'Tastiest I've had for a long time,' he replied.

Harmony's cheeks flushed at the compliment.

'Care to hear more or am I boring you?' she asked.

'Tell me everything,' Brett urged.

'Recently masked riders have been ranging up and down the valley after dark,' Harmony said. 'Previously a small amount of stock had been rustled, but these raiders started stealing whole herds. They also fired shots at homesteaders who tried to stop them. Only last week we buried Silas Long who was shot by a masked rider he caught trying to rustle every last sheep he had on his land. Silas and Meredith Long came west on the same wagon train as Tom and myself. We became good friends. I even assisted at the birth of her baby daughter.' She swallowed. 'Now my dear friend Meredith is a widow — just like me.'

'Has anyone ever seen one of these raiders unmasked?'

'Unfortunately, no,' Harmony had to admit, 'which means there's no actual proof these rustlers are Delaney's men.' Then she flared, 'But whose else would they be?' She refilled his coffee mug. 'They're organised, Brett. Very well organised.' She paused before saying, 'And as if we didn't have enough to contend with, we have Cheyenne trouble too.'

Brett stood up and walked over to her window.

He let his eyes follow the trail back up to the pass he'd ridden through. He glimpsed a small cloud of fine grey dust lingering there in the stillness.

He told her, 'I had a couple of Cheyenne riders follow me in.'

Harmony drew in her breath sharply. 'I don't suppose they were an old warrior and a young buck?'

'Describes them pretty well,' he said quietly.

She trembled. 'Could be the same two who've been here before.'

'Right here? On your land?'

'Yes,' Harmony told him, 'at least three times. Could have been more.'

'What happened?' he asked, his eyes searching the pass.

The widow recalled, 'I saw them on my land twice, riding across my range like they owned it. I just stood at the window with Tom's old rifle in my hand. I was shaking, hoping and praying they were just passing through. And that's what they seemed to do. That was a couple of weeks ago. Then, the third time was at sun-up. I woke up and opened the door. I was right in the doorway, Brett, about to go outside in my dressing gown to feed my mare like I've often done and that's when I saw these two Indians, right close to my cabin. They were the same two I'd seen before. One was thin with long grey hair. He stayed on his pony by the stable, but the other, who was indecently half-naked, was less than twenty paces from the cabin, right by the water trough.'

Brett had been listening intently to her talking while looking at the pass. Finally he saw the two Indians who'd shadowed him, resting astride their ponies, almost concealed by a bunch of arrowhead pines north on the balcony rim. They were motionless, as if carved there. He might easily have missed them but for the sun's glint on one of their rifle barrels.

'Reckon they're up there in the pass right now,' he said.

Anxiously, she asked, 'You can see them?'

'By the pines in the pass.'

'Dear God!'

'Tell me what happened when they came calling.'

'I knew what the younger one wanted

60

sure enough,' Harmony said, standing close beside him. 'I could see it on his face. Made me feel real scared.' She lowered her voice to a husky whisper. 'The kinda terror only a woman knows.'

'But you handled it?'

'Lady Luck was on my side,' Harmony told him. 'Just as things could have been getting ugly, my prayers were answered. A couple of homesteader men rode by my spread. They spotted the two Cheyennes close to my cabin so they decided to pay me an early morning visit. When the homesteader men started heading across my land, my unwelcome callers left me and rode away over the creek behind my cabin.'

'You're a brave woman, staying here on your own.'

'Some say brave, others say foolish,' Harmony admitted. 'My parents live in Pennsylvania. When they heard of Tom's death, they wrote urging me to pull up stakes, come home and be with them, but I felt then, and still feel now, that Lonesome Valley is where I belong.' She looked up at him. He still had his eyes fixed on the two Cheyennes motionless in the pass. Impetuously, she asked a curious question. 'Have you ever belonged anywhere, Brett?'

'Been a drifter most of my life, Harmony,' he replied. 'Drifter by choice.' He thought about it. 'Longest time I've ever stayed to put down my roots was almost five years in a mountain town called Buckskin.' He said wryly, 'That's where your letter caught up with me.'

'Sorry I took you away.'

'No apology needed,' Brett assured her. 'I came because I wanted to.'

The sun was no longer glinting on that rifle now as the Indian riders retreated into the pass. She breathed a sign of relief, but Brett stayed watching for several minutes before resuming his seat.

'So have the other settlers had Indian trouble too?' he asked.

'Yes, just recently,' she said. 'Last four or five months in fact. Will Quade found one of his sheep full of arrows, then Buck Jamieson, who owns the first spread you see when you come down from the pass, saw some Cheyennes trying to steal his three ponies. Buck told me he sent the varmints all packing with a hail of bullets. Then, only last week, some homesteaders swapped lead with Indians trespassing on their land. It's all strange, Brett. We've been at peace with the Indians ever since we came here. We've even traded with them. Tom once took me to their camp and bought me an Indian shawl for my birthday. I remember wearing it to church the next Sunday.' She fought back her tears. 'That was a couple of weeks before his accident.'

'Has anyone been stirring up trouble with the Cheyennes?'

'There's only one man with a motive.'

'Delaney,' he supplied.

'We homesteaders already feel under threat because of those masked riders and if the Indians keep making trouble, that will spook us even more,' Harmony told him. 'That's why many of us believe Delaney is somehow provoking the Indians — but no one knows how.' Bitterly, she added, 'But even if we found out and had proof, the sheriff in Red Butte would just sit on his big fat ass, pardon my language, Brett, and do nothing except chew the cigars Delaney supplies him with. Same goes for his useless, drink-sodden deputy too. You see, Brett, Delaney holds all the cards.'

'And you're up against a stacked deck,' he stated.

'Yes,' she said forlornly.

Brett watched her closely over the table. The future of the homesteaders in Lonesome Valley seemed bleak indeed. Garth Delaney was a crafty, ruthless adversary and it was highly probable he was behind both the masked raiders and provoking the Indians. He'd come up against low-life like Delaney before, power-hungry, relentless, evil, and many of those men were now under the earth in their local graveyards, courtesy of his twin Colts. Those guns felt very much at home against his thighs right now.

'How many men does Delaney have on his payroll?'

'At least half a dozen, but the main ones are Buff Malloy, a crazy Dutchman named Anton De Heus and Kid Jorgenson.'

Brett frowned. 'Heard of Malloy. Sneaky as they come. He shot a cardsharp in Tombstone City, gun under the table. Malloy accused the tinhorn of cheating and fired a bullet right through his gut. It was point blank range, blew him clean off his chair.' Then he raked in the money on the table and walked out, cool as you please. No one challenged him either. Haven't heard of the others.'

Harmony continued, 'Don't know much about Anton De Heus. He's rarely seen in Red Butte, but I'm told he's in charge of Delaney's business interests outside of town. Delaney has a stake in anything that makes money and De Heus is one of the few men he really trusts. As for Jorgenson, well, my husband Tom once punched him to the ground. We were walking the boardwalk outside the Dance Hall in Red Butte when Kid Jorgenson made a rather uncouth, crude remark about me. Tom took exception to it. I told Tom it didn't matter and to forget it. But Tom was so irate he hit him square on his jaw, flattening him. Jorgenson just crashed to the boardwalk. He pulled his gun from its leather but Tom's boot ground his wrist into the wood. I remember hearing his bone crack like a snapped twig. Jorgenson wailed like a baby and Tom snatched up his gun.'

'Your Tom sure had guts.'

'You two would have got on well,' Harmony said, smiling.

He agreed, 'I'm sure we would have.'

'Brett,' Harmony said, looking steadily at him, 'we homesteaders called a big meeting just over two months ago. It was held in Will Quade's hay barn. Some of the settlers were ready to pack up and quit their land. Others were seriously thinking about it. Mostly, though, they wanted to stay. We'd all come hundreds of miles with our possessions stacked in wagons to start a new life here. We weren't breaking the law. Claiming public land is perfectly legal. Why should we leave? We talked over lots of plans of action but no one could agree. The meeting looked like it was about to break up, nothing resolved, when I stood up and made a suggestion. They wondered what on earth a widow could contribute.'

She said nothing for a moment, clasping her hands.

Then she recalled, 'I told the meeting Tom and I had once met a man who was a professional gunfighter. His name was Mr Brett Cassidy. I said I'd heard he'd retired but I said that maybe, just maybe, he might still be willing to help. I told them I was volunteering to write a letter.'

Brett told himself this woman had hope and courage, more grit than many men he'd met on this far frontier had. He couldn't help but admire her.

'So they agreed?'

'Well, yes, but . . .'

'But what? They didn't all agree with approaching a professional gunfighter?'

Brett Cassidy had known this to happen in the past. Mayor Whittaker had confided in him that several members of his Town Committee had qualms about hiring what they called a 'professional killer' but they were overruled by others who were more realistic.

'A couple of settlers were concerned but in the end they agreed,' Harmony said. 'However, they were worried about — about your fee. They asked how much your fee would be. I just said I didn't know. Will Quade and some of the other men said a professional gun-fighter would cost us over a thousand dollars but when they passed the hat around later, they only raised . . .' Looking embarrassed, she had to admit, 'They raised just three hundred dollars. That's all they could afford.'

'Harmony, this one's on me,' Brett put her mind at rest. 'I'm not doing this for money. I'm here because your husband Tom once saved my life. I owe him. I owe you. That's why I rode all this way to lend a hand.'

'Thank you, Brett,' she exclaimed gratefully.

It was then Brett heard the thud of hoofs.

'Reckon you have company, Harmony,'

'I know who that will be,' she said confidently.

'Someone friendly?'

Walking to the door, she predicted, 'It'll be Will Quade, my neighbour. He and his wife Amanda have been keeping an eye on me since I lost Tom.' She reached the doorway. 'Yes,' she confirmed, 'it's Will. He must have seen you ride in and decided to check I was OK.'

Brett and the widow both stepped outside as the rider came closer.

4

Brett watched as the rider approached.

William Quade was a thick-set man with broad shoulders, bulging stomach and a bull neck. He was on the wrong side of seventy, hatless, showing a shiny bald spot right in the middle of his shaggy, unkempt grey hair. He gave the impression he was prepared for any eventuality because he was armed to the teeth.

Two rifles hung in saddle scabbards and a couple of Colt.45s rested ready in his holsters. A short-handled shovel was strapped to one scabbard and coiled rope dangled from his saddle horn. He was astride a brown gelding already streaked with foamy sweat, and he rode the snorting animal past the old wagon right up to Harmony's cabin. He glanced first at Harmony, then a little warily at the stranger.

Still in the saddle, one hand resting on a rifle, Quade leaned forward and asked anxiously, 'You OK, Harmony?'

'I'm fine, as you can see, Will,' Harmony assured her anxious neighbour.

Quade nodded. 'Just thought I'd mosey over and check.'

'I'm obliged, as always,' Harmony said gratefully.

Quade fixed his wary, questioning eyes on the tall stranger. Guardedly, he greeted Brett with, 'Howdy, Mister . . .'

The widow then introduced the gunfighter. 'Will, this is the man I spoke about in our meeting. Meet Mr Brett Cassidy. If you remember, and I hope you do, I promised to write to him on behalf of all the Lonesome Valley homesteaders. I did just that, Will. I came home, sat down and wrote that very night. Posted it from Red Butte next day. Well, the letter took a while to reach him, but here he is.'

Quade's scarred, wizened old face lit up like a beacon. Grinning, he eased his burly frame out of the saddle and planted big boots in the dust.

'You don't say! So you actually came!' He waddled towards them. He had a slight limp, legacy of a foolish act of bravado when he and his wife were passengers on a stagecoach. Outlaws held up their stage west of Carson City and Quade played the hero, groping for his gun. One of the outlaws pumped lead into his left leg. Later, on reflection in the doctor's rooms, he counted himself lucky not to have been killed.

'Just arrived,' Brett told him.

'Name's William Quade, but my friends just call me Will.'

'Pleased to make your acquaintance, Will,' Brett said briefly.

'Same here,' Quade said warmly. 'When Harmony said she'd write to you, most of the settlers thought she was wasting her time. In fact, only several in the meeting believed you'd actually come. . . .' Proudly, he added, 'I was one of 'em. True believer, that's me.' He stopped short, suddenly feeling embarrassed. Clearing his throat, he asked tactfully, 'Uh, has Harmony informed you of our financial position?'

'Not looking for money,' Brett said.

The homesteader blinked, considering. He remarked, 'That's mighty unusual talk for a professional gunfighter.'

'I'm here for personal reasons.'

'Come inside, both of you,' Harmony invited.

They followed her into the cabin. Brett elected to stand while Harmony found enough coffee brewing in the pot to pour some for her neighbour.

'Does Mr Cassidy know what we're up against?' Will Quade asked the widow as he sat down.

'He knows everything,' Harmony said.

'Well, there's something Mr Cassidy doesn't know, that's for sure,' Will Quade announced. 'It's something that might explain why the local Cheyennes are making trouble for us. They could be missing some of their women.'

'Better explain that,' Brett said.

'Let me start by saying the Reverend Jason O'Toole, the preacher in Red Butte, does some circuit riding,' Quade said. 'He preaches in his Tabernacle Church on Sunday afternoons and during the week rides out to deliver the Word to families who live out of town. Most of these folks live in Rattler Canyon, west of Red Butte. They're not homesteaders like us. Mostly they're holed up there because they've had disagreements with the law and the sheriff's not partial to riding that far out of town. Anyway, Preacher O'Toole still regards them as part of his flock.' He muttered, 'I say he's welcome to them.'

'Maybe get to the point,' Harmony prompted.

'Yeah, right,' Quade conceded. 'My wife says I ramble on too much.'

'So do folks at our meetings,' Harmony laughed.

Quade resumed, 'Fact is, I was in Rattler Canyon myself a few days ago. I delivered a milking goat I'd sold to ole man Blight and his Mexican woman. On my way back I happened to come across Preacher O'Toole who was headed home after preaching to the converted. That's when I discovered the real reason O'Toole likes circuit riding in Rattler Canyon. I could smell him a mile away.

You see, away from his wife, who's the president of the Red Butte branch of the Temperance Union, he'd been drinking red-eye with his flock and when I met him plumb in the middle of Rattler Canyon, he'd sure had more than enough. Mind you, he boasted he'd be stone cold sober by the time he got back to Red Butte but that wasn't all he said. He told me he'd had a strange vision while riding home.'

'Preacher O'Toole often has strange visions,' Harmony reminded Quade. 'A lot of folks will tell you that.'

'Well, the preacher said he'd seen a vision of some Indian women stacked in the back of a wagon. He said there were half a dozen. According to O'Toole, this wagon-load of Indian squaws was pulled by a couple of horses. It was too far away for him to elaborate but he swore he had this vision. Normally I'd take what Preacher O'Toole says with a grain of salt, maybe even half a grain, but this time I'm saying I believe he saw those Indian girls being taken away in a wagon.

Even if he was blind drunk he couldn't make up that sort of story!'

'Who was driving the wagon?' Brett asked.

'Asked O'Toole that same question,' Quade replied. 'He said there were two white men on the driving seat, but he was too far away to see their faces. He did tell me the wagon was travelling like a bat out of hell.'

'In what direction?'

'It sounds crazy, I know, but he said the wagon-load of Indian squaws was heading in the direction of Red Butte.'

Brett thought about the way station owner's warning and the ominous smoke signals he'd seen on his way here. White men stealing Cheyenne women could be the spark that fired up an Indian War and these settlers, on homesteader plots in Lonesome Valley, would be easy targets if wholesale shooting started. A really big Cheyenne raid could easily decimate the homesteaders and scare any survivors off their acres, thus giving Delaney what he wanted, public land back for extra beeves.

'I'll take a ride to Rattler Canyon in the morning,' Brett decided.

'I'll come with you,' Quade volunteered. 'I can show you where I met up with the preacher.'

'I leave at sun-up.'

'I will be here.'

The two men walked outside after Quade had finished his coffee.

'Never thought I'd meet up with a real professional gunfighter,' Quade said. He added gleefully, 'I'll let the others know.'

'Not yet,' Brett told him firmly. 'For the first couple of days I want to mosey around without folks knowing who I am or why I'm here.'

'If that's the way you want it.'

'That's the way it needs to be.'

'Sure, Mr Cassidy. You can rely on me to keep my trap shut.'

'See you at first light.'

Quade climbed into his saddle and picked up his reins. Speaking in low, confidential tones so only Brett could hear, he said, 'I know the coroner ruled that Tom McBeath's death was an accident and Harmony had to accept his finding. I suppose she thought what else could she do? And she needed some sort of closure. But I've never swallowed the accident story. Neither have some of the other homesteaders.'

Brett asked, 'So what do you reckon happened?'

'Tom had gone missing for three days. Mrs McBeath was frantic. We formed a search party. A couple of homesteaders found him at the foot of a cliff on the Wells Fargo stagecoach trail north of Red Butte. Face all smashed in, not a pretty sight, specially as a coupla buzzards had got to him. Our riders discovered his horse grazing on the cliff top. That's what convinced the coroner to make the finding he'd fallen from his saddle and toppled over the cliff.'

'So did that happen soon after he had his clash with Jorgenson?'

'Real soon after,' Quade said grimly. 'By the way, that Kid Jorgenson's still around. The rooster struts around Red

Butte like he owns the whole damn town. Flamin' upstart!'

'Anything else you want to tell me?'

'If there is, it'll keep till tomorrow.'

Quade made ready to ride back to his spread. He frowned because there was something on his mind that he felt was needed to be said.

'Uh . ... Mr Cassidy . . .'

'Yeah?'

Quade saw Harmony emerge from the cabin so he lowered his voice again and spoke quickly to Brett.

'I don't want you to take offence at this, but I've seen the way she's been looking at you. And I've noticed your eyes, too.' Bravely, he warned, 'You might be a professional gunfighter and I'm just a common ole sodbuster, but if you don't treat the widow right, you'd have to answer to me — and to my wife.'

Brett raised his eyebrows at this elderly homesteader's sudden surge of bravado. He liked the man. He had guts.

'I'm sure Harmony's a mighty respectable woman so you and Mrs Quade can sleep easy,' Brett assured him. He grinned now. 'Besides, I've ridden a long trail. The only thing I have on my mind right now is shut-eye. See you in the morning.'

5

Harmony had just lit her cabin lamp when Brett's roan let out a warning whinny from the lean-to stable. The gunfighter took three steps to the window curtains and parted them. It was sundown. Tall pines made stark arrows against the crimson sky in the twilight world of shadows. Suddenly a shadow moved, then another. There were two riders this side of the old wagon Tom and Harmony had come west in.

'We have company,' Brett said. 'Reckon our Cheyenne friends are back.'

'Oh, thank God you're here,' Harmony McBeath whispered beside him, clutching his right arm.

'Stay inside, Harmony,' Brett told her firmly, 'while I find out what the hell they want.'

'Be careful,' she whispered. 'Please be careful, Brett.'

Picking up his rifle, he edged the door

slowly open. Looking out through the thin crack between door and frame, he could only make out two riders, definitely the same ones who'd shadowed him on his way. According to Harmony, these were the Indians who had been here before. However, Brett figured there could be others concealed out there in the dusk so he was taking no chances.

'Get that rifle you greeted me with,' he said.

'Yes, yes I will,' she said, hurrying to the cupboard where she grabbed Tom's old hunting gun.

'And keep away from the window,' he warned her.

He stood motionless in the doorway, rifle in hand, his eyes roving slowly over Harmony's range. Still he saw no movement, but that didn't mean more Indians weren't there. As for the two he could see, they were etched against the fading light of day. Now he could play a waiting game, but he'd had enough of them. It was time to challenge these Cheyenne riders. He leaned his rifle against the cabin wall. He didn't want it to come to gunplay but if so, his twin Colts would be sufficient.

A night owl hooted from the high branches of a pine as Brett walked slowly towards the two mounted Indians.

They both seemed surprised to see him and exchanged brief words. Maybe they'd judged he was merely a visitor and would be gone by now. If that's what they'd thought, then Brett was doubly concerned. As Brett approached, the older Cheyenne warrior spoke sharply to the young buck, as if restraining him.

Brett halted ten paces away.

'I am a friend of the Cheyenne people,' he said in their tongue. 'I once lived amongst you and I know your lingo.'

The Indian riders both stared at him, uncertain now. They hadn't expected this. As for Brett, he was grateful for that winter in a Cheyenne camp. He'd not only learned their language, but some of their ways.

The older Indian said slowly, 'We do not know you.'

'My paleface name is Brett Cassidy,' the gunfighter stated. 'In Chief Meturato's camp I was called Hair-on-Face because in those days I grew a beard.'

The older Cheyenne considered this carefully. He was in no hurry to reply but finally he said, 'I have heard of Chief Meturato. His camp is many moons ride from here.' Thinking some more, he said, 'my name is Avonaco.'

'Leaning Bear in my lingo,' Brett informed him, still hoping to keep things on a friendly basis.

'My son's name is. . . .'

'I speak for myself,' the younger buck interrupted, his tone sharp. He leaned forward over his pony's head and said quickly. 'Ocunnowhurst.'

'Yellow Wolf,' Brett translated.

The buck's eyes narrowed. He had two weapons, a rifle in a skin sheath and a hunting knife hooked under his belt. Unlike his father, he was far from impressed this white man had spent time with his people. Rather, hot resentment blazed from his eyes.

'What are you doing here?' Brett demanded.

Yellow Wolf replied scornfully, 'Cheyenne warriors do not need to answer paleface questions.'

'But this is paleface land,' Brett pointed out.

Ignoring Brett's statement, Yellow Wolf spat into the earth.

'Where is woman who lives here?'

'So that's what this is all about,' Brett said slowly.

Leaning Bear told him, 'My son has come here to talk to her.'

Brett knew Yellow Wolf had come for more than talk. Harmony had read the real intent on his face and he could read those piercing eyes right here and now. This Cheyenne brave was on a mission. He wanted a woman and having set eyes on Harmony he desired her. If he succeeded, she wouldn't be the first white woman to be kidnapped and taken as a squaw. Twice, when he was in the Army, they'd rescued two such women from Indian villages and brought them back to Fort Glory. The women were never the same again. It wasn't going to happen to Harmony McBeath.

'My woman does not wish to talk to Yellow Wolf,' Brett asserted.

'Your woman? She is not your woman!' the Indian buck challenged. He sneered, 'You have not been here with her!'

'So you've been watching,' Brett accused.

'You lie,' Yellow Wolf insisted. 'She is not your woman!'

The gunfighter bristled, his hand itching to lift his right side gun. It would be so easy for him. Just one bullet and Yellow Wolf would be dead before he toppled from his cloth saddle. But he didn't want to make things worse between the homesteaders and the Cheyennes.

'She is my wife,' Brett said coldly. 'I have been away hunting.'

Leaning Bear nodded sagely and spoke to Yellow Wolf. 'My son wastes his time and my time too.'

But the young warrior was in no mood to listen to his father's counsel. He'd seen the white woman, more times than she knew, and he wanted her. It was more than desire. Having told other braves in his camp he would bring her home, his standing among them was at stake. Failure meant scorn from his peers.

Yellow Wolf slid snake-like from his pony's back to the ground and set his face for the cabin.

Brett barred his way.

Shaking with rage, Yellow Wolf pulled his hunting knife from his belt. Crouching, he brandished the blade as Brett stood his ground. Suddenly the Cheyenne lunged at him. Brett could have easily lifted a gun and blasted him but instead he sidestepped Yellow Wolf and grabbed his right wrist. Locked together, the two men swayed in the dusk. Brett twisted the Indian's wrist, forcing his fingers open. The hunting knife slipped from his grasp, falling between them before thudding into the dust. Old Leaning Bear never moved, merely sitting astride his pony watching as Brett rammed his knee into the younger man's belly. Yellow Wolf yelped as pain raced through him, then screamed again when Brett's two fists landed in his chest, both close to the heart. The Cheyenne faltered, tried to trip Brett with his left foot but the gunfighter hit him again, this time square on the jaw. Glimpsing his knife protruding from the earth, Yellow Wolf tried to scoop it up. However, Brett booted it clear of the Indian's grasping fingers. Straightening up, Yellow Wolf walked straight into Brett's right fist that squashed his aquiline nose. That's when he tumbled. He crashed to the ground at Brett's feet where he lay clutching his broken nose, blood oozing between his fingers.

Brett picked up the knife and walked to Yellow Wolf's pony where he lifted the ancient rifle from its sheath. Then he stood back as the battered Cheyenne buck first sat up, then clambered slowly and painfully to his feet. Brett didn't need to say anything. Yellow Wolf was not only returning to his village empty-handed, but even his weapons had been taken from him. He would take years to live this down and Brett watched as he trudged crestfallen to his pony. His body had taken such a beating it was difficult for him to mount up. In fact, it took two attempts before Yellow Wolf was able to sit on his cloth saddle. His eyes were glassy.

The sun had almost drifted below the western ridges when the old Cheyenne, Leaning Bear, left his son and rode over to where Brett Cassidy stood with the captured weapons.

Brett said, 'He needed to learn a lesson, Leaning Bear.'

'You are wearing two guns,' the old Indian observed. 'I thank you for not killing him.'

'He'll be sore but he'll be fine.'

'Tell your squaw that she will not be bothered again by my son.'

Brett assured him, 'Both of us wish to live in peace with the Cheyenne people.'

'It is good to live in peace, but white people need to stop acts of war.'

'Tell me what you mean, Leaning

Bear.'

'White men have been seen shooting buffalo and deer on our lands,' the Indian warrior said. 'That is stealing Cheyenne food.' After a long silence, Leaning Bear then continued, 'They have also stolen our women.'

'How did this happen?'

Leaning Bear said, 'Twice white men have entered our lands and taken our women. Three squaws were captured while checking fish traps in a river outside one of our villages. They were just taken. Their bodies have not been found. They must still be alive. We did not know where they were, but the men of that village started talking of war. Then, just days ago, six women, some of them maidens who have never been with a man, were grabbed from my own village. Our men were out hunting, leaving the women with some old men, even older than me. The white men came with guns. The women were forced into a wagon and taken away. When our hunters came home, they followed the wheel tracks to a big canyon. We call it Valley of Snakes.'

So Preacher O'Toole's 'vision' wasn't merely the ravings of a man who'd imbibed too much. He really had seen a wagon-load of Indian women, all taken from their Cheyenne homelands.

'Rattler Canyon,' Brett supplied.

'That is the place,' Leaning Bear confirmed. 'Our warriors entered this canyon. Many white men live there. We say Valley of Snakes is Cheyenne land. We have allowed your people to build their cabins there, but when those white men saw our braves tracking the wagon through the canyon, they forgot Cheyenne generosity. They opened fire on our warriors. Two were shot dead. Another wounded. He will walk with a limp for the rest of his days. We do not know where our women were taken. Will they become slaves, like some black-skin people we have heard about?'

'Leaning Bear, I know you speak the truth and I'm telling you these white renegades will be punished,' Brett promised.

'My people are angry, the drums of war are being heard in some villages and our young men, like my son, Yellow Wolf, are ready to raid and kill.'

'These white renegades are not the settlers in Lonesome Valley,' Brett pointed out. 'The people who live here on their small farms are peaceful.'

'Young braves painted for war will just seek to kill whites and this valley, being close to Cheyenne land, will be where they will strike first,' Leaning Bear predicted. 'Hear me, Hair-on-Face, you are a good man. But good and bad alike die in war. In last few weeks, some Cheyenne bucks have made raids on this valley, maybe taken some sheep or cattle for food, but what you have seen is nothing compared to what many young braves are planning.'

'Listen to me, Leaning Bear. I know you are a wise man. You know if there's a massacre in this valley, then the bluecoat soldiers will come in and destroy your people and seize your land. I don't want this, neither do you.'

'But if white men keep taking our squaws, nothing will stop war.'

'Father!' Yellow Wolf finally spoke up. He'd been chastened, he'd lost a fight and the anger was still there, making his voice tremble. 'When the moon is full, a war party will ride.' Defiantly, he told both men, 'I will ride with that war party.'

Brett glanced up at the rising moon. There were two nights left before the moon was full. Time was running out.

'I will do what I can to find and return your women,' Brett promised.

'Do this and we will live in peace once again.'

'So long,' Brett said.

There are no words for 'hello' or 'goodbye' in the Cheyenne tongue but Leaning Bear raised his hand in a gesture of respect. He then spoke briefly to his son and turned his pony. The young buck lingered, fixed his dark, brooding eyes on the white man, spat into the dust and joined his father.

Together they retreated, taking the track that led back to the road.

Brett opened the cabin door and saw Harmony framed in the lamp glow. She was white-faced and trembling. Still holding her hunting rifle, she ran to Brett and clutched his arm with her free hand.

'I was watching through the curtains, Brett,' she said, holding on to him. 'When he came at you with that knife, I was so scared for you.'

'They won't be coming back,' Brett said.

Harmony breathed a sigh of relief. 'You sound very sure.'

'As sure as a man can be.'

'You seemed to be doing a lot of talking,' Harmony said, her fingers finally trailing away from his arm, 'but I couldn't hear a word that was said.'

'I once learned their lingo so we all understood each other.'

'But the young buck took exception to what was said?'

'His name was Yellow Wolf and he had his sights set on you.'

She shivered. 'I knew as much.'

'I decided to put them both off once

and for all.'

'How did you do that?' she asked.

'I told them you're my woman,' Brett recalled for her. 'Well, more than that. I said you were my wife.'

A flush of red sprang to Harmony's cheeks and she gasped, 'Oh!'

'Figured that would convince the young buck he was wasting his time,' Brett explained. 'At first he didn't get the message, but he did by the time I'd taken his weapons and sent him on his way.'

She breathed an audible sigh of relief. 'I'm very grateful, Brett. I might not be your wife, but you certainly deserve some of my home cooking.'

'Looking forward to it, Harmony.'

★ ★ ★

Night closed over Lonesome Valley as Harmony cooked the evening meal. She fried cutlets of corned beef, heated potato and vegetables from her garden and bread pudding. It had been a long time since she'd entertained a guest for supper and she hesitated before reaching in the pantry for the small bottle of wine she'd been given last Thanksgiving. They shared the meal. She spoke at length about how hard it was to be a widow on a homesteader's acreage, but he sensed her determination to realise the dream she and Tom had in coming here. He said little about himself. He mentioned his army service, the year in a Cheyenne camp, but little else.

After all, what does a professional gunfighter talk about to a decent woman?

Outside, a chill wind coming down from through the pass swept across the valley, making the pine branches sway, ruffling the grasses and raising dust along the trail. Clouds edged across the face of the moon.

'You said you're meeting Will here tomorrow?' she asked.

'At first light,' Brett confirmed.

She hesitated. 'So — so you'll be staying here tonight?'

'If that's OK?'

'Yes, yes, of course it is.'

Harmony looked across the table. Brett Cassidy was seated in the glow of the lamp, drinking coffee she'd just made for him. She remembered that afternoon in Jericho Creek, remembered how she'd looked at him in that fleeting moment he'd drifted past the wagons on his way out of town. After he'd ridden past, she'd felt a touch of guilt at even looking that way at a man who wasn't her husband. She was glad no one had noticed her.

But she looked at him now, more lingeringly.

She admired him for keeping his promise to Tom. It was like he was keeping his promise to her too. Yet she was fearful. The hopes of every settler in Lonesome Valley were invested in this man. But how could one man, even a professional gunfighter, get rid of Delaney and his gang? Surely there were too many of them for one man. And no one would ride with him. Not that he would ask. In any case, none of the homesteaders had the stomach for a gun battle with Delaney's killers. The only exception would most probably be Will Quade, but he was too old, too slow. Delaney's men would fill him with lead for sure and there would be another grave and another grieving widow in Lonesome Valley.

She prayed they wouldn't kill Brett Cassidy. Despite his reputation, he was outnumbered, a man alone against a bunch of murdering swine.

'I'm glad you're staying tonight,' she said. 'Makes me feel safe.' Her eyes met his over the table. Her voice turned husky. 'Sorry this cabin is so small, Brett. There's just this parlour and — and my bed. Tom said if we had a family, he'd have to build an extra room.'

'Don't worry about me,' Brett said softly. 'I'll sleep in the stable.'

* * *

One hour later Harmony undressed and slipped into her blue nightgown.

Tom's framed picture was nailed to the wall. One of the men who travelled with them on the wagon train fancied himself as an artist and most nights he sat with paints, brushes and easel offering to sketch any man, woman or child who agreed to sit for him. At Harmony's urging, Tom agreed and she was glad. Since his untimely death, that picture had brought back many cherished memories.

It hadn't been easy being a woman alone here in Lonesome Valley.

Men had come calling soon after Tom was buried.

Mostly they were fellow-homesteaders who'd lost their wives and were looking to remarry. One man in particular, Bart Boone, a brash pioneer from Pennsylvania, had been most persistent and finally Harmony had found it necessary to rebuff him and actually tell him not to pay her any more visits. Many men simply hadn't realised she needed to be alone with her grief.

Lately, however, she had felt lonely and with the passing of time, few homesteaders, men or women, came calling to spend time with her. The exception had been the Quades. They were good people. She liked and trusted them.

She walked to the window and parted the curtains.

Her eyes drifted to the stable and she found herself thinking about the tall gunfighter bedded down there. She wondered whether Brett Cassidy was asleep or keeping watch? Somehow she imagined him fully awake, like a sentry at his post. She felt a stirring within, the kind of womanly stirring that had remained dormant since Tom's death.

Harmony crossed the floor to her bed.

She turned down the lamp wick and placed it next to her locket on the small bedside table. She slipped between the blankets and rested her head on the pillow.

There she lay awake for a long, long time and her last thoughts before surrendering to sleep were of the stranger in her stable.

6

Harmony rose while it was still dark, brushed her hair and hastily donned a dressing gown over her nightshirt. She fried eggs and bacon and called her guest inside for a quick breakfast before he left. Brett already had his roan saddled and, just as he finished his coffee, first light showed and Will Quade, true to his word, came riding in. The homesteader remained in the saddle, ready to leave.

'Thanks for the hospitality, Harmony,' Brett said.

'It was the least I could do,' she told him.

With Harmony watching in the doorway, Brett Cassidy and Will Quade rode together across her land. They joined the main valley trail. As the new day's sun poked over the far away ridges, the riders reached a cleft in the valley's southern wall. Here the trail was narrow, uneven, just wide enough for riders to travel single file. They rode slowly in the shadows until the passage widened into a ravine that in turn emptied into a long, wide basin hewn out of sandstone by countless years of burning suns, fierce winds and winter floods. It stretched almost as far as Brett could see, from towering mountains in the east to a rugged pass in the west.

'This is it,' Quade announced. 'Rattler Canyon.'

'The Valley of Snakes, according to a couple of Cheyenne visitors last night,' Brett said as they rested their horses.

'Last night!' Quade flared. 'After I left?'

'They won't be back,' Brett calmed him down.

He gave Will Quade a brief account of his encounter with Leaning Bear and Yellow Wolf.

'Thank God you were there,' the settler said, relieved. 'Harmony shouldn't be alone! My wife's been hinting again and again to Harmony that she needs a good man.' Quade's trembling fingers built a cigarette as he looked out over the canyon. 'The stories about snakes are certainly true. When settlers first arrived in this canyon they soon noticed there were more than usual here. Big ugly sidewinders, specially down by the creek where folks pan for gold. Only last week Jed McConaughey's youngest daughter, Emma, was bitten by a fat rattler sunning itself in the reeds right where she went paddling. Unfortunately she couldn't be saved. Poor kid died in less than an hour.'

'Let's look for those wagon wheel tracks.'

The homesteaders' leader took a quick drag on his cigarette and led the way down into Rattler Canyon. Its sheer walls were crumbling and half a dozen trails spilled through shadowy gaps. Cabins made mostly of stone stood like sentinels by those narrow passes. Smoke wisped from a few iron chimneys. The terrain was harsh although Brett saw patches of grass and the occasional arrowhead pine. The creek that wound through the middle tumbled over rocks and made a dozen pools.

Looking beyond this creek, Brett made out a well-worn, dusty trail.

With the new day's sun rising above the bare rims, the riders headed together across the canyon floor. They started to ford the creek when Brett saw a sidewinder curled arrogantly on the bank, right where they were headed. It didn't even look like it would slither out of the way. Riding his roan through the shallows, Brett lifted his right side Colt. A gunfighter needs to keep in practice and without seeming to aim, Brett fired at the deadly snake, blasting a hole an inch back from its head. The rattlesnake jerked, then lay still as a stone.

The riders mounted the eastern bank, rode through some high grass and came upon the main canyon trail that was pocked by hundreds of hoof prints and boot marks, testimony to its use by the settlers who lived here.

'This is where I met up with Preacher O'Toole,' Will Quade recalled as they halted their horses. 'I'd just come down from selling the milking goat to Billy Blight and his fancy senora who live in that hole in the canyon wall you can see straight ahead. Just a cave but there's furniture inside, all they need.' He sensed that Brett Cassidy wasn't particularly interested in the Blights' living arrangements, so he resumed, 'When I reached the trail here, right where we are now, I saw O'Toole on his horse, and like I told you, he was drunk as a crazy skunk.'

Brett asked, 'Which way did he say the wagon was headed?'

'West,' Quade recalled.

'Travelling along this canyon trail?'

'The preacher didn't say, but when I looked around after he'd gone, I couldn't see any wheel marks there.'

'We'll ride around and look for sign,' Brett decided.

They crossed over the trail and rode a grassy slope dotted with sage bushes.

Now Brett had never trained as an army scout, but when he'd stayed in that Cheyenne village, he'd learned plenty from his Indian friends. It was time to call upon that Cheyenne wisdom. Patiently, slowly, he allowed his roan just to drift over the grassy flat. Noticing some stalks of grass bent over and others flattened, he rode his horse closer. Reaching the disturbed grass, he halted his mount in the shadow of the canyon wall, dismounted and beckoned the settler to him.

'Wheel marks,' Brett pointed out.

'You've got an eye like a flaming hawk!'

'Tracks are about a week old, I reckon.'

'About the time I saw Preacher O'Toole,' Will Quade recalled.

Leaving the homesteader to swig water from his canteen, Brett crouched low and examined the wheel marks in more detail. At length, he pronounced, 'Tracks are deep. The wagon that made these tracks was carrying a load.'

'Like half a dozen Indian girls?' Quade asked pointedly.

'It fits.'

'Well, now! Seems the preacher had more than just a vision.'

'We'll see where these tracks lead.'

Brett swung back into the saddle and, with Will Quade riding alongside him, he followed the wheel marks west. The wagon tracks kept their distance from the well-used trail but went in the same direction. Twice the rim tracks swung around small sage-draped hillocks but each time they returned to keep heading west adjacent to, but not joining, the canyon trail. It was as if the men driving the wagon wanted to be far enough away from the main trail so a passing rider couldn't identify them. Possibly Preacher O'Toole had told the truth when he said they were too far away for him to see precisely who they were.

It was close to high noon when sheer sandstone walls squeezed the canyon floor into a narrow pass. The riders saw three willows shadowing the ford where the main trail crossed the creek. The wagon tracks too led to this same ford. Brett and Quade dismounted to let their horses drink the cold creek water. The homesteader built a cigarette, but Brett's attention was drawn to a piece of material trapped against a stone under the largest willow. Leaving his roan, Brett parted the willow's sweeping branches and picked up the torn material. It was light brown, decorated with elk eye teeth, its edges frayed like it had been ripped from a garment. Brett examined it more closely, remembering what the squaws used to wear in the Cheyenne village he'd spent time in. Then he saw another piece. It was smaller, hanging from a branch. He probed further into the willows, finding a third piece of brown material, caked with mud and wrapped around a protruding tree root.

Suddenly his boots sank into a bed of freshly turned clay.

'Will — come here,' he called.

'Something's wrong?'

'Bring that shovel you carry.'

There was urgency in the gunfighter's tone so Will Quade wasted no time. With his cigarette drooping from his cracked lips, he unstrapped his short-handled shovel, parted the trailing willow branches and tramped over to where

Brett was standing. The gunfighter took the shovel and began digging. The shovel only went down six inches before striking two small human feet. The left foot was bare, the other still covered by a brown moccasin. Rooted to the ground, staring in sheer horror, the homesteader was white-faced and shaking as Brett lifted more earth from the makeshift grave. Within five minutes, they both looked down upon a brown-skinned Indian maiden whose ruthlessly shredded dress barely covered her decomposing body. Brett carefully scraped soil from her face. There was an obvious knife wound in what was left of her breasts. She was young, probably only sixteen. Her eyes, still preserved, were wide open, frozen in utter terror as she breathed her last.

'Bastards,' Brett said softly.

'Why — why did they kill her?'

'I'll leave you to figure that out.'

Brett shovelled clay back over her corpse. When the young woman's body was covered once more, he handed the shovel back to Quade. 'You go to church,

Will?'

'Well, uh, only sometimes.'

'If you know some words to say, then say them.'

Quade frowned. 'She's not a white woman. . . .'

'Still say the words, Will,' Brett insisted firmly.

Brett Cassidy was angry. No woman, whether she was a white settler or an Indian maiden, deserved to die like this and be dumped in a wilderness grave. While Brett stood by under the willow in silence, Quade took off his hat and in a hoarse voice recited the first three verses of the Good Shepherd psalm. They were all he could remember.

When Quade had finished, Brett said, 'I noticed some flat stones by the creek. We'll pack them over the grave so the coyotes don't get to her.'

As they walked together to the creek, Quade told himself that Brett Cassidy was no ordinary gunslinger. He was tough and deadly with the gun, but there was another side to him. He liked the man and he had an idea the widow felt the same. However, Cassidy was a gunfighter. It was a pity he wouldn't be staying around.

With the grave protected by stones, the two men made their way back through the willows where they remounted their horses. They forded the creek and resumed following the wagon tracks which now ran much closer to the trail. By the time the riders reached the mouth of the canyon, the wheel marks had joined the trail itself.

The trail left the shadowy Rattler Canyon and followed the widening creek down across a boulder-strewn plain. They passed two cattle ranches, signed Bar Y and Rolling B, both well-established, here well before the homesteaders had arrived. The second ranch had its owner's name crossed out and in its place were the hastily-scrawled words:

NOW OWNED BY
GARTH DELANEY

Not content with just owning the Lazy F Ranch and having his sights on the whole of Lonesome Valley, Delaney was extending his empire this side of town too. They rode by an old abandoned trading post and a sheepherder's hovel, both crumbling by the side of the trail. Cresting the next ridge, they saw the town of Red Butte sprawled below them. Here they were not only on a ridge top, but at a fork in the trail. There were two signs nailed to a post. One was freshly painted, indicating the obvious trail to Red Butte, the other was faded, like it was of no account. This sign pointed to a very narrow track that curved around a lonely butte to Lonesome Valley.

'I'm obliged to you for taking me to Rattler Canyon, Will,' Brett thanked the homesteader. 'Saved me a lot of time.'

'I can stay with you,' Quade offered.

'No, Will,' Brett said firmly. 'You ride back to your wife. Take care of her, look after your land.' There was a coldness in his eyes as he looked down at Red Butte.

He said slowly, 'This is my game from now on.'

'Been a pleasure to ride with you.'

'So long, Will.'

Leaving the homesteader leader to take the track home, Brett set his face for Red Butte. Harmony had told him the town was originally an army outpost built under the almost sheer red slopes of a small hill. The outpost, put together hastily, had long been deserted by the cavalry and a town had been born where once blue-coat soldiers practised their marching drills across the parade ground. The town had prospered, its citizens living in peace — until the day Garth Delaney had ridden in.

Brett rode closer to Red Butte. He could still plainly see the wagon marks in the dust until the tracks from Rattler Canyon met two other trails, one used by stagecoaches from the east, the other heading away to the south. The three trails converged right on town limits and the wheel tracks Brett had followed all the way from Rattler Canyon suddenly merged and mingled with a dozen others and a hundred boot marks. Besides all this, the flat was churned up by cattle and horse hoofs. This then was trail's end as far as the wagon tracks were concerned.

So where had the Cheyenne maidens been taken? Could they be in Red Butte, which lay just ahead? If so, surely someone would have seen them. Or could they be in one of the other towns where Delaney had 'business interests'? It was highly unlikely the kidnappers had taken their captives along a major stagecoach road to another town. Wells Fargo drivers and passengers might see what they shouldn't. If they weren't in Red Butte, they would surely have been taken somewhere else along back-trails. There was no way of knowing for sure where the wagon and its human cargo had gone from here. But he was going to find out and he'd start with the town that spread before him.

And so Brett Cassidy rode in, slowly,

just as he'd ridden into many other frontier towns in the past — on a mission to kill. He rode past cattle yards and sheep pens, then headed his roan into First Street, the town's spine, from which alleys sprouted like small bones. Distant hymn singing reminded him this was the Sabbath and the faithful would be gathered in their churches. In fact, the first building he came to was the Red Butte Tabernacle Chapel, a small stone building with a bell tower. The singing had ceased and instead the preacher's sermon rumbled like thunder out over the street. The bright blue sign out the front told passers-by that the Reverend Jason Micah O'Toole was the church's minister and all were welcome to worship at 3pm every Sunday.

O'Toole's booming exhortation to righteousness assailed the gunfighter as he drew adjacent to the chapel. He sounded extremely sober this afternoon! Brett decided it was a good time to have a friendly chat to the man who had visions, but he wasn't inclined to attend his church.

Instead, he drew his horse under the shade of a juniper and waited.

7

Brett stayed in the saddle for more than half an hour while Preacher O'Toole admonished his congregation about the sins of the flesh. In strident, forceful tones, he warned about the evils of gambling, drinking, cussing and in particular the sin of fornication. His fist-thumping of the pulpit almost raised the roof. Mercifully, his sermon came to an end as the sun began to retreat over Red Butte. The robust singing of the final hymn followed by the benediction rang out over the town, then the porch door was pushed open. The Reverend O'Toole, a large black-bound Bible tucked under his arm, emerged first, followed by his smiling wife.

They positioned themselves to shake hands with the faithful.

O'Toole was tall and lanky, towering over his petite wife. His neat, barber-cut hair was the colour of ripened corn, well clear of the collar of his starched white shirt. A spotted blue bow tie sat below his bobbing Adam's apple. He wore a sombre black suit and matching boots. Mrs Tabitha O'Toole, already chatting dutifully with two Temperance Union members from her husband's congregation, had red hair poking out from her Sunday bonnet, just stroking her long, home-sewn blue dress. Her face wore a perpetual smile.

It was Tabitha who saw the rider first.

Nudging her husband who was delivering an embarrassingly loud second sermon on the evils of 'living in sin' to a young couple who were yet to be married, she pointed out the stranger under the juniper tree. Sensing another possible recruit for his growing church, Jason O'Toole smiled in eager anticipation, left the faithful and marched like a soldier across the street.

'You're a bit late for church, brother,' he boomed.

'Actually, I heard most of your sermon,' Brett said wryly.

'I preached a little longer than usual today,' O'Toole said. He explained sanctimoniously, 'Many sinners needed to be brought to repentance.'

The congregation were watching, but obviously no one knew the rider and he'd never met up with any of them before either. That suited Brett right now.

Brett said, 'From what I heard, you're a man who speaks his mind. I'm impressed.'

'Praise the Lord and thank you,' O'Toole said, beaming at the compliment. It was always good to receive confirmation of his gospel ministry. He rubbed his hands together and announced, 'My name's . . .'

'It's on your signboard,' Brett pointed out.

'Oh yes, of course.' O'Toole asked, grinning. 'And you?'

'Name's Cassidy.'

'Are you just passing through or staying in our fair town, Mr Cassidy?'

Brett didn't get to answer because right at that moment Tabitha O'Toole decided she should join her husband and welcome this stranger. She excused herself from the fervent conversations about the evils of the demon drink and started to walk across the street. She'd just reached the middle of First Street, when without warning, two riders came thundering out of the alley alongside the church. Tabitha was right in their path, meaning both men had to rein their horses hard to avoid crashing straight into her. In fact, one of the horses actually brushed her, knocking her off balance. O'Toole, running out of the juniper's shade, caught her in his outstretched arms before she slipped over.

While Tabitha clung to her husband, sobbing, the rider whose chestnut horse had sent her reeling, sat in his saddle glaring at her. He was young, barely into his twenties, with little curls of dark hair making an excuse for a beard over a sallow face that was dominated by thin eyes, bloodless lips and flared nostrils. He wore a single pearl-handled gun, slung low on his left side.

'The street's for men and horses,' he upbraided the preacher's wife, 'not for day-dreaming fillies.'

'Don't you talk to my wife like that,' O'Toole addressed him furiously.

'I'll talk to your wife any way I like, Preacher,' the rider mocked him as his congregation looked on nervously. He raised his voice deliberately, so everyone could hear, 'And you'll do nothing about it.'

'Why, you . . .'

'Jason, for God's sake, leave it,' his wife whispered.

But the rider heard it and laughed. 'Yeah, sound advice, ma'am. You're a smart lady!' He grinned at O'Toole. 'Do like your wife says, Preacher.'

The rider's companion, a beefy man well into his fifties, chuckled loudly at the preacher's embarrassment.

'Who the hell are you?' Brett demanded.

Both riders fixed their hostile eyes on the stranger in town as he nudged his horse out from the juniper's shade. At the same time, Preacher O'Toole took advantage of this momentary diversion to rush his wife safely back across the street where his congregation stood in bewildered silence. Two Temperance Union ladies looked shocked and someone called for smelling salts. Being church day, none of the men wore guns. Not that any would be game to use them if they did.

'Name's Jorgenson,' the younger rider stated. He smirked and asked arrogantly, 'Heard of me, Mister?'

Brett ignored the question. Instead, he said, 'This is Sunday, day of rest and peace, Jorgenson. These folks have just come out of their church. Reckon they've a right to cross the street without getting knocked over.'

Jorgenson stared at him. He wasn't used to being challenged in Red Butte and he took an instant dislike to the stranger's tone of voice and his attitude.

'Wanna make something out of this?' Jorgenson taunted.

'I'm suggesting you slow down so no

one gets hurt,' Brett said in a quiet, reasonable voice.

Jorgenson's eyes narrowed to twin slits.

Provocatively he sneered, 'You goddamn interfering polecat . . .'

'Kid,' his beefy sidekick intervened, as one of the church ladies looked like she was about to faint, despite the smelling salts, 'this isn't the time or place for a ruckus.'

'Stay out of this, Buff,' Jorgenson snapped back at him.

Buff reminded Jorgenson, 'We're wasting time. We've both got important work to do for Mr Delaney.'

Jorgenson considered, finally agreeing, 'Yeah, you're right, Buff.'

'Come on, let's ride,' Buff urged.

Jorgenson couldn't resist a parting shot as he gathered his reins. Looking straight at Brett, he warned, 'I'll give you a piece of advice, stranger — if you want to stay healthy, keep riding.'

Brett made no reply, watching as the two Delaney men rode off in a swirl of dust. He'd heard all about Kid Jorgenson, first from Harmony and then from Quade as they rode together. He was every bit as hot-headed as they had described. The other was obviously Buff Malloy. Brett figured he would be meeting them both again but not in front of a church congregation.

'Thanks for horning in, Mister,' O'Toole said, coming back to him. 'My good wife is particularly grateful and she wants me to invite you to our humble home for light refreshments. We live in the stone house next to the church.'

'Sure, I'll spend some time with you, but no preaching.'

'Agreed,' O'Toole said with a grin.

Brett tied his horse to the picket fence. The preacher's home was squeezed between the church and Venetta's Hat Shop. It was indeed humble, just a parlour, bedroom and office. Tabitha was an artist and her paintings of mesquite and sagebrush hung on the parlour wall.

There was something else hanging on this wall, too — a John Brown Sharps

Carbine. Brett thought it was an unusual adornment in a preacher's home, but it was none of his business.

'You were most definitely sent by the Lord, Mr Cassidy,' Tabitha insisted as she busied herself at the woodstove.

'If you say so, ma'am,' Brett said, taking off his Stetson.

'Men like Kid Jorgenson and Buff Malloy are the scourge of our community,' the preacher's wife said bitterly. 'They belong to Garth Delaney's outfit. They've ruined this town. Red Butte was once a decent place to live in but now no man, woman or child is safe here.'

'And no one dares to face up to Delaney's crew,' O'Toole lamented.

Now Tabitha O'Toole might have given the appearance of being meek and mild but when it came to Delaney and his gang, she couldn't help but raise her voice in anger. Much of what she then said Brett had already heard from Harmony and Will Quade and she backed up all their concerns. However, half way through her tirade she seemed to

125

suddenly remember she was a preacher's wife and needed to observe some decorum in the presence of their table guest.

'I'm sorry, Mr Cassidy,' she said, pouring tea for him. 'You're new in town. Probably just here for the day. I shouldn't have burdened you with our troubles.'

'No need to apologise on my account,' Brett said.

'So are you just passing through?' Jason O'Toole wanted to know.

'I'm here to make some enquiries.'

Curious, Tabitha asked, 'Are you one of those Pinkerton detectives?'

'Fact is, I'm making enquiries about some missing persons.' Brett took a quick sip of Tabitha's tea while looking straight at her husband. 'Actually, half a dozen Cheyenne maidens. I aim to track them down and return them to their people. Might prevent an Indian War.'

Both the preacher and his wife exchanged glances and fell silent.

Right then all the fire seemed to go

out of Tabitha and she slipped a reassuring arm around her husband's shoulder. Meanwhile, Preacher O'Toole's face was turning chalk-white and he looked old and gaunt.

'You've been talking to Will Quade?' O'Toole guessed.

'We rode together to Rattler Canyon,' Brett informed him.

'So he told you about my vision?'

Tabitha explained, with a touch of pride, 'The Good Lord often gives my husband visions, Mr Cassidy.' She hesitated. 'However, in this particular instance, I felt it was more than a vision. It was real life. My husband actually saw that wagon and he shared what he'd seen with Mr Quade.'

'Will told me about it.'

'However, at the time my head was banging like a drum,' O'Toole confessed. 'I was unwell so I couldn't remember much.'

Brett saw Tabitha involuntarily raise her eyebrows and in that moment he figured she knew of her husband's embarrassing secret. Maybe she'd been protecting her preacher husband for years.

'You could help me out by telling me what you do remember,' Brett urged.

The preacher went over the story he'd blurted out to the homesteader leader but Brett learned nothing new.

'What sort of wagon was it?' the gunfighter prodded.

O'Toole thought about it. 'Reckon it was one of those big Conestoga wagons that new westbound settlers use to cross the plains in. Very heavy, too heavy for the two horses so that's why the whips were cracking.' Frowning, the preacher recalled, 'The canvas was torn in lots of places so I saw the Cheyenne women quite plainly, all huddled together, scared as . . .'

'Scared as hell,' Brett supplied.

'Uh, yes,' O'Toole agreed.

'What about the horses?'

'Like I said, just two.'

Brett asked, 'Anything special about them?'

'One was brown, very ordinary, the other a real big chestnut.'

'Like the one Jorgenson was riding today?'

Tabitha interrupted hastily, 'My husband's not saying, Mr Cassidy.'

'What about the two wagon drivers? Who were they?'

'Jason has told you enough,' she said, sharply this time.

This preacher knew who they were sure enough, and he must have confided in his wife, but Brett saw naked fear written plainly on their faces. These were good, God-fearing folks and, like most other decent citizens in the town, they were scared of crossing Delaney's men.

Brett Cassidy decided not to probe any further, apart from one last blunt question. 'Have you seen these missing Cheyenne maidens here in Red Butte?'

'Good gracious, no,' Tabitha answered quickly and very definitely indeed. 'We would have certainly heard if they were here.'

129

'Thanks for the tea and cakes, Mrs O'Toole.'

Leaving her husband at the table, Tabitha O'Toole accompanied Brett to the front door. As he stood in the doorway, the preacher's wife let her eyes drop to the guns he wore. The holsters were made of polished leather and the gun handles were shiny-clean. He'd said he wasn't a Pinkerton man. She couldn't imagine he was a lawman, which left few other possibilities, one of which caused her to shudder.

She couldn't be sure and she certainly wasn't going to ask him, but he possessed all the cold characteristics of a professional gunfighter. Tabitha hoped she was misjudging him. The very idea of a man who killed for a living made her sick in the pit of her stomach.

And yet, she asked herself, would it take such a man to rid this town of its resident evil?

Thinking about this, she watched him walk to his horse. She kept her eyes on him as he mounted up. Briefly, he just sat in the saddle looking out over the town, which was bathed in brilliant sunlight and late-afternoon shadows.

As he gathered his reins, he glanced back at the distant slopes behind Rattler Canyon. That's when he saw Cheyenne smoke, dark puffs drifting into the fading sky, a reminder that time was running out.

Then, as Tabitha O'Toole closed the door, Brett Cassidy began to ride.

★ ★ ★

The preacher's wife returned to the parlour and drew in her breath sharply as she saw Jason holding the carbine he'd just taken down from its wall hooks.

'Don't even think about it!' she warned.

O'Toole muttered, 'Who said I was thinking about anything?'

Tabitha blazed, 'I've been your good, faithful wife for almost fifteen years, Jason Micah O'Toole, and I know you through and through. You can't hide anything from me.' She spoke more softly now, 'Not even your drinking.'

'Fact is, I was just remembering,' the preacher said, still nursing the lethal gun.

'You need to forget those misspent years with John Brown,' she admonished him. 'He might have led an antislavery crusade, with the best of intentions but many men died in that battle of Harper's Ferry.'

'And this gun killed some of them.'

'Some say the battle of Harper's Ferry led to the Civil War,' Tabitha reminded her husband. She added earnestly, 'But, Jason, the past is the past. You're a man of God now, a preacher of peace.'

'Not easy to preach peace when the likes of Delaney, Jorgenson and Malloy are raising hell in your town,' Jason O'Toole mused.

'We have to leave it to the Lord,' Tabitha insisted. Inexplicably, impulsively, she thought again about that tall stranger, Brett Cassidy, and how he'd just ridden into their town. There was something about him that moved her to say, very quietly now, 'I'm sure the Good Lord has it all in hand.'

'Yes, my dear, you're probably right,' her husband agreed.

The Reverend Jason O'Toole lifted his old carbine back on to its wall hooks.

8

Brett Cassidy rode slowly down First Street.

All was quiet, like a ghost town, as he passed by the Tabernacle Chapel and the Quaker Meeting House set back under some pines, but further into Red Butte a few shops were open and folks walked or lounged on the wooden-planked boardwalks. It was easy to see who owned this town. There were two bakeries, both with Delaney's name painted on their signs. The boot shop was owned by Delaney, as was the gaudy-fronted 'Black Deuce Card House'. Judged by the haze of cigarette smoke in the doorway and the line of horses outside, the card house was well-patronised. Brett slowed his roan as he rode by the general store and the Red Butte law office where the open door showed him a stout town sheriff with his boots planted on his desk, puffing away on a fat cigar and reading the *Red Butte*

Herald. Beside him, a much younger deputy was drinking coffee.

Half way down the street now, he heard the tinkling of piano keys and the tune 'Darling Nelly Gray', then outbursts of raucous laughter greeting him as he came closer to the town's one and only saloon.

Originally the army outpost's barracks, the Last Chance Saloon took up a whole block on First Street. Riding closer, Brett saw four dusty windows, two either side of bright blue batwings. A dozen lanterns hung over the boardwalk, ready to be lit at sundown, and the saloon was flanked by Corporal Alley and Sergeant Alley, two more reminders of the old bluecoat days. The town's lodging house was right opposite the saloon. He noticed the carefully and artistically printed name 'Ma Tully' had been almost scraped off its door and hastily replaced with 'Delaney' scrawled untidily in vivid blue.

The afternoon shadows were deepening as Brett crossed the street and dismounted at the tie-rail. Tabitha O'Toole's cup of tea, although appreciated, wasn't really his style and besides, he'd always found a town saloon to be the best source of information. It was time to poke around inside this one, especially as it was owned by Garth Delaney.

He let his roan drink from the water trough.

Inside, the piano player was being applauded for 'Darling Nelly Gray'.

Someone yelled, 'Give us Old Dan Tucker!'

Brett glanced down-street. Most of the smaller businesses there seemed to have escaped Delaney's greedy clutches, but the one on the other side of Corporal Alley was a freight line with DELANEY'S FREIGHT plastered in big blue lettering over a signboard. It looked to be closed today, but a freight line meant wagons so he'd take a look around there later.

He tied the roan next to three other horses and mounted the boardwalk.

Half-naked saloon girls painted crudely on the four dust-coated windows smiled seductively at him as he walked to the batwings. It might be the Sabbath and very early afternoon, but Delaney's saloon was over half full. Three men stood drinking at the bar counter. One had his left arm around a painted saloon girl's shoulder. She wouldn't even be sixteen, too young to be in here. Other painted cats, a little older, but mostly still in their teens, sat playfully on the laps of any men who could afford their company. There was a faro game in the far western corner, half a dozen poker games were being played and three men were talking earnestly over drinks at their table under the balcony.

Two of those men were the riders he'd tangled with, Kid Jorgenson and Buff Malloy.

From the description Harmony had given him, the third man, heavily-built, dressed in a pin-striped suit, had to be Garth Delaney. He had a high forehead, bushy black eyebrows and a long, thin nose. None of these three men were drinking redeye whiskey like most of the others in the saloon. Instead they were enjoying glasses of imported red wine.

Brett let the batwings creak to a standstill behind him.

For a long moment no one noticed him, then the saloon girl playing 'Old Dan Tucker' looked up from her music with her fingers frozen on the piano keys.

'Well now! Look who we have here! Mr Brett Cassidy!'

Jessie May Killen rose from her piano stool and smiled. It was a smile from long ago, many years in fact, all the way from Lincoln City. It was a smile that brought back certain memories. The years had been kind to her. She was well past her prime, but still looked vivacious, her eyes very beguiling and her lips full and inviting. She was wearing a red cotton saloon frock sewn together tight enough to accentuate and give a glimpse of the swell of her ample breasts.

'Howdy, Jessie,' Brett greeted simply.

Brett was conscious that Delaney,

Malloy and Jorgenson had ceased their conversation and were all looking his way. Watching the newcomer with narrowing eyes, Delaney raised his glass of wine slowly while his two men simply stared. Jorgenson's lips were curled in a sneer and he was leaning forward over the table, crouching, like he was ready to leap out of his seat.

'Welcome to Red Butte,' Jessie proclaimed enthusiastically.

She said it so loudly the whole saloon was plunged into silence. Men looked up from their drinks and the faro banker stopped shuffling his cards. Brett took half a dozen paces and she met him half way to the bar counter. He could smell her European perfume and now she was close to him, he saw how her powder and paint tried to cover the lines on her face. However, she was still a beautiful woman.

'Been a long time,' Jessie said.

'Seven years, I reckon.'

'Buy me a drink, Brett,' she invited.

'Thought you'd say that,' he said.

'Nothing changes, Brett. You know that.'

Jessie May Killen was once the undisputed highest-paid and most sought-after queen of Lincoln City and that's where he'd met her. She'd worked in the Lucky Cowboy's Palace owned by Jim Wiley who'd hired him for a kill. Wiley's brother had been stabbed to death in his cell by a rogue lawman who subsequently had his badge taken away from him by an angry town. Jim Wiley wanted the trigger-happy ex-lawman in a pine box and so he sent for gunfighter Brett Cassidy. He recalled earning those seven hundred and fifty dollars in full view of the town by out-drawing and killing him with a single bullet between his eyes.

'I'll have a whiskey,' Jessie said at the bar. He recalled with a wry grin she used to boast she was able to drink any man under the table. Maybe she still could. He told the bartender, 'Make it two.'

'What are you doing in Red Butte?' she asked.

'I was going to ask you the same question.'

'Long story, Brett.'

'I'm listening,' he prodded.

'After you left Lincoln City, I hooked up with Jim Wiley. Then Lucille his wife cottoned on and I no longer had a job. Found myself a good man in the next town. He was the bank manager, but he was shot dead in a hold-up. Two masked men just busted into the Cattlemen's Bank and shot him at point blank range. I told the townsfolk they ought to hire you, but the law caught up with them before they got around to writing the letter. Hung them both from a cottonwood tree.' She signalled the bartender for another shot of whiskey which Brett paid for. 'I was down on my luck, working in places I don't care to talk about, when I met Garth Delaney. He brought me here and set me up here, in his Last Chance Saloon. I figured it was my last chance, too, so I've made the best of it.'

'I'm sure you have.'

'I'm not just a common saloon whore

here, Brett,' Jessie said. 'I sing, I play the piano, I have my own room and I'm in charge of all the saloon girls. I don't have to accept any old cowpoke's company. If a man's dirty, he has a bath before he's alone with me and he pays for the bath, too. I set my own prices and Mr Delaney takes a percentage.' She smiled at him, softly now, a smile he knew from long ago. Playfully, she offered, 'However, for an old friend like you, it would be half price, maybe even less.'

'Your memory's not so good, Jessie,' Brett said.

Jessie's smile faded. 'Oh, that's right, I remember now. Brett Cassidy never pays for a woman.'

'You remember right,' Brett confirmed.

And of course, Jessie told herself as she looked Brett Cassidy over once more, he didn't need to.

All the same, she felt a trifle annoyed at his rejection. She'd had men fight over her; she'd had range riders spend a month's paydirt for thirty minutes alone with her in Room Two. Only last week some very eager beavers who lived in Red Butte boasted they'd even given up drinking whiskey so they could save up for ten minutes with the Last Chance's saloon queen. It mattered not to Delaney. Even if he was missing out on his whiskey profits, he took a substantial cut from every interlude in her bedroom.

But Brett Cassidy wasn't like them, she thought furiously.

He never had been.

'Have it your way,' she snapped. 'You always did.'

Jessie had a short temper and she tapped her fingers on the bar counter in frustration. She didn't like it when a man rejected her, even if it was for a good reason. It trampled on her pride. Brett looked past her. Delaney was still seated at his table watching him like a dangerous hawk, Malloy was pouring himself another glass of wine, but Kid Jorgenson had reared to his feet. Smelling trouble brewing, Brett watched Jorgenson drift towards the bar counter.

'So what are you doing here, Brett?' Jessie demanded.

'Just passing through.'

'You're never just passing through,' she remarked sharply.

'We once had a good time in Lincoln City but that's in the past,' Brett said. 'Now stop prodding me.' He suggested, 'Find yourself a customer.'

'Damn you, Brett Cassidy!'

Jessie turned away from him, her elbow spilling her whiskey which slopped over her saloon dress. She swore like a trooper and then saw Jorgenson standing just a few paces away. And by the fire in his eyes, the Kid was spoiling for a fight.

The saloon girl stepped back from them both.

'So do you two gentlemen know each other?' she asked.

'Me and the preacher-lover have met,' Jorgenson confirmed.

'Preacher-lover?' Jessie exclaimed, laughing.

Brett leaned back against the bar counter, cold eyes appraising Jorgenson whose fingers were flexing.

'I was considering teaching that crazy loon, Preacher O'Toole, a lesson, when this stranger interfered in what was none of his damn business.'

'He's no stranger to me,' Jessie said.

'Mr Delaney, Buff and me were watching you,' Jorgenson spoke up. 'We figured you must have known him.'

'I'll introduce him,' Jessie said as the whole saloon listened. 'This is Mr Brett Cassidy, the famous gunfighter. I saw him in action in Lincoln City, saw him beat a man to the draw and shoot him right between the eyes. Killed him on Main Street with half the town watching on. You see, Mr Cassidy has a reputation.'

A murmur floated through the Last Chance Saloon. Card games and the pouring of drinks were temporarily halted. A very young saloon girl, suddenly very nervous, slid from a patron's lap and ran under the balcony to her room.

One old timer, whose grey beard

reached way down past his waist, piped up with, 'Yeah, sure I've heard of him. He's a professional! I reckon he killed the Barkley brothers. Mind you, those two varmints got what was coming to them. Good riddance, I say.'

Having heard Jessie and the old timer talk about Brett Cassidy's reputation, Jorgenson faced him squarely.

Brett saw eyes glittering in anticipation. He'd seen men with eyes like this before, men eager to enhance their own reputation by beating a professional gunfighter to the draw, or by getting him to back down. It didn't matter which, but with most young upstarts the preference was to kill. And Kid Jorgenson's face had 'killer' written all over it as he stepped slowly towards the new man in town.

'So what is a famous gunfighter like you doing in Red Butte?' the Kid asked in a mocking tone.

'None of your business,' Brett said slowly.

'Working for anyone in this town?'

146

Watching, Jessie suddenly regretted what she'd broadcast to the whole saloon. Sure, she'd been annoyed at Brett. How dare any man knock her back! It was a blow to her self-esteem, but reflecting now, she didn't want Brett Cassidy shot dead on her account. After all, they had history between them. There had been good times, even though they were long ago. Looking at Jorgenson, whose eyes were brimming with confidence, she now worried the Kid was younger, maybe, yes maybe, even faster. She needed to pour water over the simmering coals.

Breaking the silence, Jessie blurted out, 'Mr Cassidy told me he was just passing through.'

Irked by her interruption, Kid Jorgenson nevertheless kept his eyes fixed on Brett as he addressed Jessie in a sneering voice, 'Button your lip, woman.'

'Like I said, it's none of your business, sonny,' Brett repeated slowly. There was a hardening edge in his voice as he said, 'Calm down and have a quiet drink.'

But Jorgenson wouldn't be denied his

intended prey. In any event, he couldn't afford to walk away. Delaney, his boss, was watching, so were many of the townsfolk, not to mention a bunch of young guns from the Lazy F who looked up to him. To merely cool off and have a drink would mean he'd drop in their estimation.

Jorgenson's left hand edged lower.

'No one tells me what to do.'

'I just did, sonny,' Brett Cassidy said, 'and I'll give you another piece of advice.' Now his tone went suddenly cold as he warned, 'Don't drop your paw any closer to that gun.'

Jorgenson's fingers lingered, hovering one inch above his Colt.

'Heard about you, Cassidy,' Jorgenson drawled. 'I was in Jericho Creek playing poker with a couple of friends when your name came up. They said you'd retired, put away your guns. I reckon, though, you're all washed up, a has-been.' Smirking, he challenged, 'Of course, if you want to prove me wrong . . .'

Brett knew where this was leading.

He'd been through all this before with other young roosters in other towns, would-be gunfighters wanting to carve a notch and make a name for themselves. Jorgenson was just crazier and bolder than most. Deliberately, Kid Jorgenson edged his left hand lower until the tips of his long, spidery fingers actually touched his leather holster. Grinning provocatively, he stroked the pearl handle of his six-shooter, then lifted it — just an inch.

But he didn't even clear leather.

Brett's draw was lightning fast, a single swoop of his hand and his Peacemaker was firing from the hip. Sudden thunder rocked the Last Chance Saloon as Brett's bullet shattered the bone in Jorgenson's upper left arm, snapping it from his shoulder. Yelping in pain, blood soaking his shirt, Jorgenson danced in agony then crashed headlong over a poker table with his gun spilling to the sawdust-covered floor. Screaming profanities, Jorgenson clutched at, then lost his grip on the blood-spattered table and slumped to the floor where he lay writing like a fish out of water.

He was next to his unfired gun. It was close to his right hand. Too close.

Brett's boot took away any temptation Jorgenson might have felt by kicking his notched gun clear. White-faced, Buff Malloy clawed his own gun but Delaney restrained him with a quick, quiet word.

Meanwhile, Brett bent over and scooped up the Kid's Colt.45.

'Bartend,' he broke the stunned silence.

A little moustachioed man wearing a stained white apron over his check shirt and black pants left the faro table where he'd been serving drinks and scampered like a scared dog back behind the bar counter.

'Yes, yes, Mr Cassidy?'

Brett tossed him Jorgenson's gun.

The sweating bartender, shaking like a leaf, caught the weapon with both hands.

'Keep this gun for Kid Jorgenson and give it back to him when he grows up,' the gunfighter said.

'Certainly, sir,' the barman stammered.

Meanwhile Jorgenson, still mouthing foul expletives, squirmed in the sawdust on the floor, his fingers desperately trying to stem the blood flow.

Brett addressed the saloon, 'Someone take this young fool to the doc.'

Two Lazy F riders looked directly at Delaney who gave them a brief nod. They ran over to the wounded Jorgenson, lifted him to his feet and escorted him out through the batwings. Delaney rose to his feet and nodded to Jessie who hastily resumed her place at the piano and started playing 'Old Dan Tucker' again.

Brett stood at the bar counter as Garth Delaney approached him.

Far from seeming hostile at Brett's shooting of his man, Delaney was smiling. It was an oily, almost friendly smile.

'Nice shooting, Cassidy,' Garth Delaney paid the gunfighter a compliment. 'I'd like us to have a friendly chat. Fact is, I could use a man like you.'

9

Brett Cassidy appraised the man who owned Red Butte. In his immaculately-tailored suit and necktie, Garth Delaney could easily be mistaken for a bank manager. He certainly looked the part. Unlike Jorgenson and Malloy, he didn't appear to be armed. He wore no guns in holsters, although Brett figured that under his suit there could easily be a concealed weapon. He'd known tinhorn gamblers to be like that — no visible guns but a deadly derringer loaded and hidden in a waistcoat pocket. So Brett wouldn't be fooled.

'I'm partial to friendly chats,' Brett said.

'Good, very good, Cassidy,' Delaney said, still smiling. 'Name your drink and it's on me.'

'A beer will be fine,' Brett decided.

'You heard Mr Cassidy,' Delaney told the bartender.

'Yes, indeed,' the bartender said, still shaking.

Just then the batwing doors burst open. The portly sheriff Brett had seen relaxing with his boots on the desk and a cigar wedged between his lips now swaggered inside, closely followed by his wiry, wide-eyed deputy. The sheriff clutched a Colt Walker revolver in his right hand while the deputy, looking even more nervous than the bartender, used both hands to carry a rifle. Two pairs of eyes ranged over the saloon.

'What the hell's going on?' the sheriff boomed.

'We heard a gunshot,' the deputy said, backing up his boss. 'Then I saw Mr Jorgenson outside the doc's surgery and a trail of blood leading back to this saloon. So we assumed . . .'

'Ah, good detective work, Deputy Caine,' Delaney complimented him in a semi-mocking tone. 'One day you'll wear the big shiny badge.'

The quip brought a round of raucous applause from the saloon patrons and

Deputy Caine actually beamed in appreciation.

Then Garth Delaney addressed the town sheriff. 'It's really good you responded so quickly, Sheriff Tremelling. Shows this community their town is in good, safe hands. However, in this particular instance, you can both calm down. Fact is, two men had a minor disagreement, a shot was fired and Kid Jorgenson has been taken to our esteemed medico, Doc Applegate, to be patched up. He'll be fine, back at work tomorrow I reckon.' He added, 'Nothing much to it.'

'Well, if you say so, Mr Delaney,' Tremelling acquiesced.

'Yes, I say so, Sheriff,' Delaney repeated slowly.

If ever Brett Cassidy needed confirmation who ran this town, here it was. Even the town's law officers were subject to Garth Delaney whose smile was fast becoming very smug. Here was a man who was obsessed with power. His word was law, accepted without question. It wouldn't surprise him if these lawmen even received pocket money or other perks from him.

'Then we'll return to office duties, Caine,' Tremelling told his deputy.

'Wait,' Delaney commanded them. 'On your way out, collect a bottle of whiskey from my bartender. On the house, of course. Take the bottle back to the law office. It'll help you with your duties.'

'Thank you, Mr Delaney, sir,' Sheriff Tremelling said respectfully.

The sheriff collected their bottle and both lawmen parted the batwings and left the saloon. At Delaney's word, Jessie's fingers began to caress the piano keys once more, card games resumed and drinks were served over the bar. Brett told himself this man who owned the law and most of the town was going to be a formidable opponent. At this moment Delaney couldn't know he was working for the Lonesome Valley homesteaders, so maybe it was time to take advantage of his ignorance because one day soon he'd be sure to find out. He would play his cards carefully.

'I'm impressed,' Brett said to Delaney.

'That's good,' Delaney said, pleased with his remark. 'Now for our chat. We'll talk in my office. Follow me.'

Brett saw how the saloon patrons all stepped aside for Garth Delaney as he strode across the floor. He noticed too that Buff Malloy was scowling. Ignoring Malloy, Brett caught up with Delaney and walked with him stride-for-stride under the balcony where there were five closed doors. The first one was Delaney's office; the others with signs 'Mature Jessie', 'Honey Hannah', 'Irena' and 'Cleopatra' were the rooms where his saloon girls plied their trade. Delaney unlocked his office door and made straight for his polished mahogany desk where he sat down and waved the gunfighter to a cushioned chair. Brett glanced at Delaney's desk. It was heaped high with papers and piles of money. He noticed the bill of sale for the lodging house. The price was a pittance but it was countersigned by Ma Tully. Right by the bill of sale was an official deed, still in her dead husband's name but probably not for much longer. Delaney just hadn't gotten around to fixing it yet.

The bartender came in with Delaney's wine and Brett's beer.

'Close the door on your way out, Simon.'

The bartender obeyed and shut the door on the saloon noise.

'I'm not a man to waste time so I'll get straight down to business, Cassidy,' Delaney said. 'You said you were impressed by the way I run this town. Well, you impressed me too. When the Kid prodded you, I wasn't sure what you'd do but you treated us all to some mighty fancy shooting. The Kid was a fool, got what he deserved. He was lucky not to be on his way to Boothill.'

'I didn't shoot to kill.'

'Figured it was that way.'

'Where is this leading, Delaney?'

'When I heard Jessie say you were Cassidy, I remembered that name and a story that was going around at the time. Reckon I heard it six, maybe seven years ago. It was a story about Hangman's Bend, where a professional gunfighter named Cassidy killed a certain Seth Wallace.'

Brett recalled the killing sure enough. Like the last assignment in Jericho Creek, he'd been hired by the Town Committee. Wallace had virtually taken over Hangman's Bend single-handed and the town was cowering in his shadow. There was a litany of crimes to his name, including murder, rape and theft. No one dared to stand up to him, especially as he'd attracted two young hellions as his sidekicks. That was until Hangman's Bend hired Brett Cassidy. The gunfighter's first bullet, right through Wallace's heart, ended his evil reign. The hellions moved on even before Wallace's body turned cold.

'That gunfighter was me.'

'Story said you were paid three thousand bucks.'

'More actually.'

Delaney raised his eyebrows. 'I'm sure you were worth it.'

'I always gave value for money.'

'You said 'gave'?'

'I retired a couple of years ago,' Brett said flatly.

'Heard that too,' Delaney said. He leaned back in his chair and fixed his eyes on Brett. 'But you've obviously lost none of your talent, Cassidy. That draw in my saloon was the fastest I've seen — and I've seen a few in my time.'

Brett shrugged and took a swallow of his beer.

'So what are you doing in Red Butte?' Delaney asked pointedly.

'Reckon that's my business,' Brett said, watching Delaney's eyes narrow at his blunt reply. 'However, I'll give you my answer. I'm just passing through.'

'Damn shame.'

'Why do you say that?'

'Well, I could use a man like you,' Delaney said slowly.

It was what Brett Cassidy had hoped he'd say, but he didn't intend to appear too eager. 'For what exactly?'

'To look after my interests.'

'And you have considerable interests. Noticed your name all over town.'

'Small fry,' Garth Delaney dismissed his Red Butte businesses as if they were of little account. 'I own a very profitable freight line that transports supplies and other goods between here and a dozen towns, in particular Gorman's Flat and Panhandle. I have business interests in both towns. Then there's Wildcat Camp, that's a mining hole, four hours ride from here. I have a thriving enterprise there. Of course, I own the Rolling B ranch and the Lazy F in Lonesome Valley. Right now I'm looking to increase my Lazy F herd, but some lousy two-bit homesteaders are in the way.'

'Sodbuster vermin,' Cassidy remarked, shrugging.

Delaney bared his tobacco-stained teeth as he smiled again. 'I like your attitude, Cassidy. Yes, sir, I sure do. We'd get along fine, real fine.'

'Like I said, I was just passing through,' Brett told him. He fixed his eyes on Delaney. 'However, if you're thinking about making me an offer to stick around, make it a good one.'

Delaney appraised the gunfighter. 'I can't pay what you earned in Hangman's Bend, but I can pay good regular money . . . with benefits.'

'Keep talking. I'll listen and consider,' Brett said.

'Well, consider this, Cassidy,' Delaney urged. 'Two hundred dollars a month, your own room paid for at the lodging house and free grub. Then, on top of that, drinks in the Last Chance Saloon are on the house.'

'You've just about convinced me.'

'And,' Garth Delaney said, 'if you join my outfit, I'm offering a special signing-on present. One of my Last Chance saloon gals is yours for the night. Jessie, who you're obviously acquainted with, will select one for you.' Smirking, he lit a cigarillo. 'I'm sure you'll enjoy the soiled dove she picks. It'll probably be Josephine, real young and pretty.'

'Actually, I'm partial to Indian girls,' Brett hinted casually.

Delaney frowned before saying dismissively, 'We don't have any here.'

'Then I'd settle for Jessie's choice.'

Garth Delaney took the cigarillo from his lips and demanded, 'So do we have a deal, Cassidy?'

'You've just hired yourself a new gun,' Brett Cassidy said slowly.

Delaney's smile broadened as he silently congratulated himself he'd just added a worthy addition to his outfit. Having Cassidy's guns to back up his other men would make him even more feared and powerful. He rubbed his hands together in anticipation of the future. For his part, Brett wanted to wipe that smile of triumph off Delaney's smug face but that would have to keep. Right now he needed to play the part of Delaney's new recruit, which should give him the chance to poke around relatively unhindered. He needed to find those Indian girls. He was certain now they weren't here in Red Butte. Of course, the word that he was actually working for the homesteaders was bound to get out, sooner rather than later, so he had to work fast.

'Any questions, Cassidy?'

'None I can think of right now.'

'You'll be working with Buff Malloy,' Garth Delaney informed him. 'Buff's my right hand man, been with me for years. He don't say much but he's reliable and you'll get along fine with him.' He hesitated before saying, 'You've already met Jorgenson. Now the Kid won't be real happy I've put you on the payroll, but he'll learn to live with my decision. Besides, in his condition he won't be itching to tangle with you too soon.'

'I can handle the Kid.'

'Book into the lodging house now. Tell Mrs Tully, the woman I bought it from, that you can have Room Five. That's the best one, even has a bath that doesn't leak. Not that you'll be sleeping over there tonight. You'll be in a saloon gal's room and if Jessie picks the redhead, Josephine, you won't get much sleep. She's young and by all accounts, very obliging.'

Brett grinned. 'I'm going to like working for you.'

'Right now, relax, have a few drinks with Buff,' Delaney told him. 'Get to know him, Cassidy. You and him will be saddle-pards.'

'First I'll stable my horse.'

'My men have free use of the livery stable, right behind the freight line office,' Delaney told him.

'I'll leave my roan there now.'

'This afternoon you drink and make merry, tonight you'll have fun, tomorrow you'll start earning your keep,' Delaney predicted as Brett opened the door. He said ominously, 'I have a very special assignment for you in the morning.' He dismissed his new recruit with, 'We'll talk about it at sun-up. See you then, Cassidy.'

Brett left Delaney's office, watched by Buff Malloy who was leaning on the bar counter. He walked through the saloon to his waiting roan.

Once Brett had left the Last Chance, Delaney emerged from his office and motioned Malloy to join him at their usual table under the balcony.

'He's one of us now, Buff,' Delaney informed him.

'Figured you'd sign him on.'

Delaney said, 'He could be a real asset.'

Agreeing, Malloy remarked, 'Haven't seen any man clear leather so fast.'

Delaney said warily, 'However, we don't really know him, Buff.'

'Thinking the same thing myself,' Malloy agreed.

'So keep a real close eye on him.'

'You can rely on me, Mr Delaney,' Buff Malloy promised fervently.

'I know that, Buff. That's why you've been with me so long.'

★ ★ ★

Brett untied and led his horse down Corporal Alley.

He passed the stone walls of the freight line office and found the gate to the fenced back yard. Shoving open the gate which whined on its rusty hinges, he saw the yard packed with wagons, close to twenty of them. Most were small freight wagons with no canvas and no iron hoops. All of them had Delaney's name painted on their sides. He glanced at a chuck wagon and several one-horse farm wagons. Leading his horse towards the livery stable, which was on the northern side of the yard, he noticed two big Conestogas. One had ripped canvas. He led his roan between two freight wagons to the livery stable. Inside were seven horses in their stalls. He noticed a big chestnut. After unsaddling his roan, he walked him to a spare stall. Draping his saddle over a stall rail, he returned to the yard.

There was no one around so Brett threaded his way through the wagons to the far corner where the Conestoga stood with its torn canvas fluttering in the swirling northerly wind. Unlike the other wagons, which were coated with fine dust, this Conestoga was caked with dry black mud. He climbed inside the big wagon and looked around. It smelled of whiskey but appeared to be empty. Then, just as he was about to climb down, the wind whipped up the shreds of dirty canvas that littered the wooden floor.

That's when he saw the moccasin.

He went over, crouched and looked closer.

The moccasin was brown, the same size as the one he'd seen on the left foot of the Indian girl who'd been brutally murdered and buried in that shallow grave. This moccasin would have fitted her right foot perfectly. It had to have been hers.

There was no doubt in Brett's mind that this was the Conestoga used to transport those captive Cheyenne maidens and its tracks had led right to Red Butte.

But where were the Indian girls now?

Delaney had said flatly he didn't have any here. He hadn't heard any saloon talk about them, not even a mention. Besides this, Tabitha O'Toole was emphatic they weren't in town. He told himself you could hardly hide a bunch of Cheyenne maidens in Red Butte. Yet they had to be somewhere. Delaney had boasted about his profitable enterprises in Gorman's Flat, Panhandle and Wildcat Camp.

They could be in any of those towns or in none of them.

Maybe he'd have to ride to all three, but time was running out.

Dusk was fast closing in over Red Butte as he climbed down from the wagon and headed back to the alley. He would act like an exemplary new member of Delaney's outfit. Accordingly, he checked into Red Butte's lodging house. Delaney had bought out Mrs Tully but he'd put her on his payroll. She was a bright-eyed, grey-haired widow well into her fifties. Her businessman husband had been a part time gambler; sometimes he'd won, sometimes he'd lost. One day he'd won this lodging house in a high stakes poker game. That was a year before he died of a frontier fever. The lodging house had been their pride and joy and she'd inherited it. She'd have still owned it now, except Delaney had put pressure on her to sell. Mrs Tully showed her new guest to Room Five. It contained a single wooden bed with pillow and blanket, table, chair and the bath Delaney had mentioned. There was a square of torn yellow carpet on the floor.

She regarded him dubiously. 'So you're working for Mr Delaney?'

'That's what I said.'

Her eyes gravitated to his twin guns. 'Means you get special treatment.'

'So I've been told.'

'I'm not really complaining about Mr Delaney,' the widow thought it best to say, as she gave his table a last dust with an old rag, 'he's been reasonable to me since I gave in and accepted his price for the lodging house.' However, Brett caught more than a hint of resentment and bitterness in her voice as she continued, 'Less than a quarter the price it was worth, mind you, but what Mr Delaney wants, Mr Delaney gets. That's the way it is in Red Butte.' She relented, 'However, he gave me a job and let me live in one of the rooms.' Her eyes stayed on those holstered guns. 'But I just wish the killing would stop.'

'Thanks for showing me my room, ma'am,' Brett said, accepting the key.

He waited at the window while she returned to her desk in the foyer.

From where he stood, he could see the full length of First Street. Kid Jorgenson had just left the doctor's rooms. His left shoulder was heavily bandaged and his arm in a sling. Flanked by the two Lazy F cowpokes who'd escorted him to the surgery, he was grumbling and stumbling back along the boardwalk on the other side of the street.

After building and smoking a cigarette, Brett left his room, crossed the street and followed Jorgenson into the Last Chance Saloon. He parted the batwings and saw Buff Malloy at the bar holding up his empty glass for a refill. Jessie glanced up from her piano playing and he caught her seductive smile. Meanwhile, Jorgenson was about to throw a tantrum, demanding to be dealt into a poker game. His face was screwed up in pain and Brett noticed bloodstains marring his sling. The Kid should probably be resting up in bed but he was making a statement by being here regardless. Heading past Jessie towards Malloy, Brett ignored the Kid's dark scowl.

Buff Malloy picked up his freshly-charged glass.

'Delaney suggested we get acquainted,' Brett said.

'Yeah, we'll be working together,' Buff Malloy agreed in a cautious but conciliatory tone. He turned to the bartender. 'Beer for Mr Cassidy.'

'Yes, yes, of course,' the bartender stammered. 'Coming up, Mr Cassidy, sir.'

Buff Malloy wasn't Brett's idea of congenial company, but a friendly chat had been Delaney's edict so he went along with it. They talked and had a beer together. Malloy told him he used to work on a southern plantation keeping slaves in order but with the Abolition of Slavery, his job ended. He played poker all along the Mississippi and casually confessed what Brett already knew — he'd killed a tinhorn. Consequently, he'd ridden west and was hired by Garth Delaney. During his second beer, he extolled the virtues of working for Delaney and Brett made no argument.

'I'll call the Kid,' Malloy said.

Jorgenson first ignored, but then responded to Malloy's beckoning finger and slouched over to join them. The Kid's face was dark as a thundercloud but with great reluctance he acknowledged the new recruit.

Brett asked, 'No hard feelings, Kid?'

Jorgenson stared at him with cold, steely-blue eyes that spoke of utter loathing and the desire for revenge. However, with great difficulty, he mouthed, 'No, none at all.'

10

It was sundown over Red Butte and Brett Cassidy was finding it hard to shake Malloy and Jorgenson who seemed on a shared mission to be with him every minute. He played along with them, suffered their profane, boring company, but he needed to be free of them and search for the captive Cheyenne girls. After tonight there was but one night left before the full moon, when according to Yellow Wolf, the Cheyenne war drums would start throbbing their messages of death. He had to get those Indian maidens safely home — but first he had to find them.

The three men were served buffalo steaks by one of Delaney's saloon girls, the redheaded Josephine. According to Delaney, she was bound to be the one Jessie would choose for his 'signing-on' present. She was young, not even out of her teens, with an ample bosom and full sensuously-pouting lips, well sought after by the woman-hungry cowpokes who frequented the Last Chance Saloon.

Brett wasn't even remotely interested, but going to her room would get him away from these two leeches. An hour drifted by and Brett's patience was finally rewarded.

Malloy and Jorgenson settled down for a game of poker with the two Lazy F cowhands who'd already had too much to drink and were exchanging sharp words with each other. One blonde-haired saloon girl slipped on to Malloy's lap and Jorgenson even invited Brett Cassidy to join them.

He didn't need to make a decision because Jessie stopped playing the piano and swayed up to him.

'Come with me, Brett,' she invited.

Unsteady on her feet, she walked ahead of him to Room Two, right next to Delaney's office.

Buff Malloy looked up from his cards. He was jealous. He'd been with Delaney for years, but he'd never been invited to

Jessie's room. Neither had Kid Jorgenson. They both hoped the new recruit wasn't going to get favoured treatment all the time. Muttering, they looked back at their poker hand while Jessie ushered Brett inside and closed the door.

Jessie lit an ornamental wall lamp and its mellow glow spread over her luxuriously-furnished room. He was standing on deep-piled wall-to-wall Persian carpet. The double bed boasted red satin sheets and matching pillows. He saw a narrow wood-grained wardrobe and a large glass-fronted cabinet displaying bottles of wine and glasses.

She sat on the bed and beckoned him. He could smell her heady French perfume and breath laden with alcohol. She was very seductive, yet tonight he was repulsed by her.

'Garth told me to pick a woman for you,' she said.

'And?'

'I picked myself,' she said, giggling.

He asked, 'Aren't you Delaney's personal possession?'

'You know me, Brett,' she said, pouting. 'I belong to no man.' She patted the bed impatiently. 'Tonight though, I'm all yours, courtesy of Garth Delaney.'

'We have plenty of time,' he said.

'All night,' she confirmed.

He glanced at the window, which was draped with long white lace. With Malloy and Jorgenson set for a long night playing poker just outside the door, he'd need to slip out through that window.

'First though,' Brett said, taking off his Stetson, 'we'll have a drink or two.'

'Or three,' Jessie chuckled.

Brett opened the wine cabinet's glass door.

Remembering Lincoln City and her weakness for imported champagne, he selected a bottle and poured her a full glass.

'So pleased you're working for Garth,' Jessie said, gulping down her champagne.

He noted her hand was shaking. She'd already had far too much alcohol, which had always been her style. Rather than sipping delicately, she drank too quickly. Not that he minded right now.

'I'm not sure what I'll be doing, but it's regular pay.'

'Mr Garth Delaney's a — very big important man — around here,' she said. Her voice was becoming slurred. 'You'll be protecting — his many business — interests.'

'So Delaney said. Tell me about them.'

'Let's just — have — a good time,' Jessie pouted, one hand holding her trembling glass, the other reaching behind to try and unhook the back of her saloon frock.

'No need to rush, we have all night.' He topped up her glass. 'Do you think I'll be working in Gorman's Flat?'

Jessie struggled with the hook. 'No, Brett, darling. That's just a quiet — peaceful cattle town. Less than — fifty souls. Not even a saloon or a card house. Garth owns the sheriff and — and the general store there.' She swore, 'Damn it! Help me get out of this — flamin' outfit.'

'Just let me finish my drink.'

Jessie's head was swimming. 'Well hurry . . . you've hardly had a drop.'

'What about Panhandle?' he asked.

'Could be where he'll — send you,' Jessie said, not winning her battle with the hook. Finally, she wrenched hard and the hook parted with the fabric. 'Mining town west of here — Garth has a big store there — been some trouble with two brothers — who had the damn nerve — to open a rival store.'

'What else is there?'

'Nothing much, darling. You won't have — any fun there. You'll just be takin' care of those — two brothers, uh, Wayne and Hyman Oakley — both Mormons.'

'Wildcat Camp?'

'That mud hole!' Jessie laughed.

Brett asked, 'Why do you call it that?'

'Big storm, river overflowed — coupla weeks ago,' Jessie said, taking another swallow of her champagne. 'Streets flooded, the whole town turned into a mud hole.'

He thought about that Conestoga with

the moccasin on the floor, the torn canvas, the smell of whiskey — and wheels and sides caked with dry mud. Those Cheyenne maidens had to be in Wildcat Camp.

'Tell me about Wildcat Camp,' he urged.

'Not much — to — tell,' Jessie said, her frock falling away from her shoulders. 'Just a two-bit mining town. Mr De Heus looks — after Garth's interests there.' She shivered, 'Don't like De Heus. He's real — mean. Ugly too.' She reached for him with her free hand, fingers linking with his. 'I'm sure Garth won't send you there. Dutchie De Heus looks after — Wildcat Camp.' She squeezed his hand. 'Now, Brett, honey, let me look after you ...'

'Been looking forward to that,' Brett Cassidy said. 'I'm all yours after one more glass of champagne.'

'I'll drink to that,' Jessie said, raising her half-empty glass.

He opened a second bottle of champagne and filled her glass to the brim.

Sitting next to her on the bed, he took a couple of sips from his own glass. Five minutes later she had her eyes closed while she guzzled more champagne. Another ten minutes and her words of seduction were so slurred no man would understand them. Brett wasn't listening anyway. He pulled her to him and she rested her head on his shoulder. Her alcoholic stench was overpowering. She dropped her glass, spilling the remaining contents over her dress. She was dead to the world, lost in her alcoholic numbness. He reached past her and pulled back the top satin sheet. He picked her up and she purred like a contented kitten as he laid her on the bed and pulled the sheet over her fully-dressed body.

Brett headed to the door and listened.

He heard the sounds of saloon patrons drinking and talking. The Last Chance Saloon was still packed.

He used Jessie's big brass key to lock the door.

Next he turned down the lamp until the room was in darkness.

Jessie was fast asleep as he walked past the bed and parted the lace curtains.

He unhooked the catch and gently opened the window. It was a tight squeeze, but Brett Cassidy managed to worm his slim body through the frame. His boots touched the dirt of the saloon's back courtyard. All the other windows had their curtains drawn across. There was no light on in Delaney's office. Either he'd gone home or he was in the saloon with Malloy and Jorgenson. There was only one window lit up and he heard the ribald sounds of Josephine entertaining a customer.

Brett walked quietly across the courtyard into Corporal Alley. There were a couple of drunken cowpokes slumped against the freight line office side wall. They were the two Lazy F hands still continuing their argument. Brett was a mere shadow in the night as he slipped silently further down the alley.

Brett opened the gate slowly, noiselessly.

Swiftly he wove his way between the

wagons and made the livery stable. Once inside, he strode to where his roan was waiting patiently. It took him less than two minutes to saddle his horse and tighten the cinch. He mounted the roan and rode through the wagons to the gate. The Lazy F hands were now trading insults, neither looking his way as he turned his horse's head down-alley.

He rode swiftly out of town, past darkened homes and empty sale yards until he came across the trail that led due south.

According to Delaney, Wildcat Camp was four hours ride.

He aimed to be there soon after midnight.

11

Leaving the lights of Red Butte behind, Brett Cassidy let his roan have his head. The big-hearted horse broke into a long, easy lope and then a steady gallop along the lonely trail that stretched south over long, flat sagebrush plains. Ahead, there was a rugged pass between two mountains, both capped with moonlit snow. He passed a couple of cabins, then a small ranch where the bunkhouse was wreathed in darkness. He forded a bubbling creek and kept on the trail that followed a new fence line holding in two more cattle spreads.

After an hour's hard riding, he rested his horse.

Within minutes, Brett was in the saddle again.

The trail began a steady climb off the windswept plain and one hour before midnight he reached the crest of a long rise. Looking down, he saw the distant lamps of Wildcat Camp. Even at this late hour, the town was ablaze with shimmering lights that cast a yellow glow over a wide river brimming against its banks. This river was like a glittering snake, twisting around the town before booming through the pass into pitch darkness.

The two mountains towered high into the starlit sky as Brett kept to the narrow trail that now slewed down towards the mining town. Approaching Wildcat Camp and the pass, he heard the dull thunder of the plunging river punctured by the sudden snarl of a gun echoing over the town. A shaft of moonlight showed gaping holes in the western escarpment. He saw thin tracks made by miners that clung to the mountain side.

The trail into Wildcat Camp dropped to the river bank.

Riding by the swollen river, Brett passed hastily-erected cabins and clusters of tents where miners had staked their claims, hoping to ride away rich one day.

He saw where the river had spilled

over its banks in the recent storm and from there the trail he rode was a muddy quagmire. The roan's hoofs squelched in deep mud, which as Jessie had told him, looked to flow right into the town itself.

He heard distant music from a tuneless piano as he rode by a bullet-pocked sign announcing WILDCAT CAMP. There were two more signs. One pointed to the western mountain and announced DELANEY'S COPPER COMPANY. Another told all and sundry there was gold along the river. Right now it would be difficult to fossick there, so he figured those prospectors smitten by 'yellow fever' would be spending time in town making traders richer than they themselves would ever become.

It was certainly Delaney's kind of town.

Brett slowed his mount as he reached town limits. So far he hadn't come across a living soul since leaving Red Butte, but he finally saw movement as he reached the head of Wildcat Camp's one and only street, a ribbon of black mud spawning a dozen very thin alleys. There was a dark ridge under the eastern mountain where wooden homes had been built behind the main street. Mostly those homes were in darkness as they presided over the town's swaying lamps.

It might be close to midnight but Wildcat Camp was very much alive.

Brett had been in many frontier outposts in his time, but few as wide-open as Wildcat Camp. The boardwalks were littered with drunks who'd passed out after imbibing too much cheap, redeye whiskey. In fact, he could smell how cheap and rancid the rotgut was as he rode by the first saloon. He drifted past two hairy prospectors having a fist fight watched by bleary-eyed onlookers from the Two Jacks Card House. Three general stores were still open for business, as was Delaney's Firearms, the town's prominent gun shop. Even the undertaker's parlour had a light burning and its front door open wide. Maybe death was a common occurrence at any hour here. He glanced down the alleys as he passed by. Some were mere unlit black holes; others held more saloons and card houses. There was once a sheriff here but now the law office was all boarded-up, its cracked windows and bullet-holed door silted with dry mud. No one had worn a tin star in Wildcat Camp for a long time.

Brett kept riding.

A woman who'd be well into her fifties stood waiting in the doorway of an obvious brothel that had the words 'Kate's Cats' scrawled over its wall. A smaller plaque informed customers this was a 'Delaney Enterprise'. She beckoned to Brett as he rode by, screeching an obscenity because he paid no notice. Just past her was a rickety wagon with 'Delaney's Freight' painted in blue on its side. It was on this wagon that another of Kate's Cats, even older than the one in the doorway, sat swinging her legs trying to entice a customer. A young mule, shivering in the cold wind, stood in harness, ready to pull the wagon away when the old saloon whore decided she'd had enough and it was finally time for some shuteye.

It was just after riding by the whore on the wagon that Brett Cassidy saw a crude, red-lettered sign hanging from a rope strung across the head of Lode Alley.

INJUN GALS $10 for 10 MINUTES

He looked past the sign and saw another, nailed above a mud-crusted window. This announced the 'Painted Woman Shebang Never Closes'. Brett ducked his head as he rode his horse under the hanging sign. He came across a dozen horses secured to a hitching rail that blocked the alley. Two of them, a flashy chestnut and a black gelding, wore Delaney's Lazy F brand.

The stench of stale cigarettes, whiskey and unwashed men assailed him as he slipped from the saddle and tethered his roan. The Painted Woman Shebang had no windows, no batwings, just an open doorway that looked like it had been hacked out of the log wall.

After tethering the roan, he walked to the crude opening.

Brett stood there for a long moment, letting his eyes rove over the makeshift saloon. Moths fluttered around the three wall lamps that provided dim light. One of the lamps spluttered. A moth smacked into its hot glass. Thick cigarette smoke clung to the roof. The Painted Woman Shebang was packed wall-to-wall with miners hunched over poker hands and whiskey glasses. Prospectors were three deep along the bar counter. He couldn't see a single saloon girl, but scrawled in red paint over the mirror behind the bar were the words, '*See Anton to book your Injun Gal*'.

He remembered what Harmony had told him. Anton De Heus was the crazy Dutchman who worked for Delaney. This had to be trail's end.

It was a town with a transient population, with men pouring in almost daily to stake claims and no one even afforded Brett Cassidy a second glance as he threaded his way to the bar. There was nothing unusual about a newcomer and to the men of Wildcat Camp, this tall man packing two guns was just another stranger. And Brett himself didn't recognise a single face.

Fronting the bar counter, the gunfighter waited his turn.

The busy man hovering behind the bar was lean and gangling, eagerly pouring drinks and stashing cash into a wooden drawer. Unlike most in this saloon, he was clean-shaven and actually wore a well-tailored dark suit that would be more than passable in church. But this was no church. This was a den of sin. Brett wasn't concerned about drinking and gambling; he'd enjoyed both in his time, but he drew the line at stolen Indian maidens being forced into prostitution.

'I want to speak with Anton,' Brett said.

'That's me, Anton De Heus.' the man behind the bar told him. He had a definite Dutch accent. 'What's on your mind, Mister?'

'Your Indian girls,' Brett said simply.

De Heus matched his grin. 'It's like the sign says, stranger. Ten bucks for ten minutes. Put your ten bucks on the bar and have yourself a good time with a real young Indian maiden.'

Brett wanted to ram a fist right into the Dutchman's mouth and shatter those gleaming white teeth, but he restrained himself. It was far more important to get those Cheyenne girls safely out of here. He didn't want to cause a commotion here and now and in addition, he had no idea who worked for De Heus in this saloon. The Dutchman could have half a dozen cronies with loaded guns sitting at tables. Dealing with the Dutchman in full view of this crowded saloon could bring more trouble than he cared to handle right now. Accordingly, he counted out sixty dollars and slapped them down in front of the wide-eyed Dutchman.

'I want a full hour and no interruptions,' Brett demanded.

'Yes, sir, indeed,' De Heus said eagerly,

raking in the money with his long, tapering fingers. Chuckling, he said, 'A man like you deserves the best and that's what you'll get. Yes, the very best.' He bellowed above the din. 'Josh!'

Anton De Heus drummed his fingers impatiently on the counter top as he waited for a bearded runt to squeeze past three poker games on his way to the bar. Meanwhile he appraised this stranger who hadn't offered his name. Not that this was unusual in Wildcat Camp. His eyes drifted to the stranger's twin holstered guns, slung lower than most. Here was no prospector! Not that it mattered, De Heus told himself. However, he was curious.

Finally, the runt fronted the bar.

'Josh, introduce this customer to our very best gal.'

'Reckon that'd be Chameli?'

'Yes, Chameli,' De Heus confirmed. Smirking, he addressed the gunfighter. 'Enjoy yourself. Josh will let you know when time's up.'

'Follow me, stranger,' Josh said.

The runt sneezed into the sawdust and threaded through the seething mass of tables, chairs and bodies to a thin door in the far corner alongside the bar counter. There was no handle. Josh just booted the door open and stumbled through with Brett right behind him. There was but one light in this crammed brothel. A solitary lamp hanging on a wall hook gave out a pallid glow, barely enough to show him a bunch of Indian girls huddled on cheap blankets strewn over the floor. Hanging curtains made six cubicles to give customers a semblance of privacy. There was no back door, no windows, not even a chair. Josh kicked the door shut with his heel.

'Chameli!' Josh summoned the tallest girl. 'Come here, squaw!'

Slowly, reluctantly, a willowy Cheyenne maiden rose to her feet. She was bronze-skinned with long black hair that hung like string past a face that was once beautiful. Now, however, Chameli's face was marred. Her left cheek bore scratch marks and the half-closed eye on that side of her face was surrounded by puffy redness. Despite what had happened to her, her right eye blazed defiance.

'Broke in this Injun filly myself,' Josh boasted proudly. 'Mind you, took a bit of rough handling but it was worth it.'

'So you beat her up?'

The runt grinned. 'Yeah, you could say that. Enjoyed every minute.'

Brett cleared leather with a swoop of his hand. Josh gaped as the Peacemaker rose in the stranger's clenched fist and he didn't even have time to cry out before the steel barrel smashed into his face. Crumbling, the runt dropped to his knees, then blacked out when Brett's gun hammered the back of his head. He pitched forward and lay still as a stone on the brothel floor.

There was one cubicle in use and the shocked customer poked his head between the curtains.

'Come out here,' Brett commanded him. 'Now!'

The ancient prospector obeyed instantly, pulling the curtain from its rails as he stumbled away from his intended prey. She was the youngest of the Indian girls, retching violently as she sat on the floor hugging her knees.

'Don't shoot, Mister!' the customer pleaded, looking down the barrel of Brett's levelled gun. He lied, 'I didn't hurt her! I promise! I hardly touched her . . . ,' 'Get down on the floor, right beside this other maggot.'

'Yes, yes! But don't shoot!'

Still pleading for his life, the old timer flopped like a whale beside Josh.

Stooping, Brett relieved him of his six-shooter and took Josh's derringer.

Then Brett spoke slowly and clearly in the Cheyenne tongue.

'I'm a friend of Leaning Bear. I've come to take you all home.'

For a moment there was disbelief. They'd been so ill-treated, so degraded by their captors and then by many of their customers, that most of them had become resigned to their fate. But as they stared at the tall man they'd never seen before, their utter despair suddenly turned to hope. He might be a white man but he spoke their lingo and he knew one of their most revered warriors! And he was offering them freedom from this vile bondage.

At Chameli's prompting, the Indian maidens scrambled to their feet. Many of them were bruised, mostly their clothes hung in shreds. They were wild-eyed, the youngest two were weeping. One had cigarette burn marks on her cheek. Unlike the percentage girls in the Last Chance Saloon and most other watering holes Brett had known, these Indian maidens had been treated like dirt. There were eight of them, five had just arrived days ago, the other three, the ones Leaning Bear had told him were kidnapped by their fishing traps, had been here for some time. They all reeked of men's sweat and the mice droppings on the floor.

'Who knows how to use a gun?' Brett silenced their excited talk.

Chameli pushed her way to the front. 'I, Chameli, can shoot.'

Brett handed her the old prospector's six-shooter. 'Who else?'

'Asha,' Chameli nominated the youngest girl who'd been forced to service the ugly old prospector now prostrate on the floor.

'You take this,' Brett offered Asha the derringer.

The young Indian maiden snatched the gun from him and immediately pointed it at her client. 'Asha knows how to kill.'

'No, Asha,' Brett said firmly.

Chameli cried out, 'Asha, this white man has come to help us. Obey him!'

Asha spat at the prospector who'd abused and hurt her.

Brett addressed them. 'I'm going to open this door and we'll walk out of here. I'll be in front. The rest of you follow in a line. Chameli and Asha, you'll make up the end of the line. If you see any man going for his gun, shoot to kill.' He directed, 'Now follow me.'

Brett Cassidy stepped to the door. The girls were bewildered, scared of the possible consequences of following this man out through a hostile saloon, but he claimed to know Leaning Bear, someone they trusted. That had to be good enough. And what was the alternative? A miserable life and possibly death from disease in this brothel? They held their breath as Brett eased the door open.

With his loaded guns in both hands, he stepped into the saloon.

At first no one noticed him. The miners were all engrossed in drinking and poker playing. It was so late some were even asleep on the floor.

Brett fired one shot into the wooden bar counter, plunging the saloon into silence.

'I'm taking these girls home, where they belong,' the gunfighter announced to the stunned prospectors who were like statues. 'If you want to keep breathing, stay right where you are. Any fool who goes for his gun gets a bullet. That goes for you too, De Heus.'

'Who are you? You're crazy!' Anton De Heus fumed from behind the bar.

Brett ignored De Heus and took three steps into the saloon with the first two Cheyenne girls right behind him. Seething, De Heus swore like a trooper and clawed at the rifle he kept concealed under the bar counter. The Dutchman's long fingers clutched the gun and lifted it clear, but Brett's twin Colts fired in deadly unison, pumping two bullets into his chest. With blood oozing through his shirt, Anton De Heus dropped his rifle, staggered back against the mirror and collapsed over a shelf full of drink bottles. Dead on his feet, De Heus crashed to the floor with bottles splintering around him.

'Anyone else for Boothill?' Brett asked.

No one spoke. No one moved.

Every customer in the Painted Woman simply stared incredulously as this stranger marched deliberately through them, booting chairs and tables aside, elbowing two drunken prospectors out of his way. The Indian girls followed him, most of them clinging to each other. Chameli and Asha brought up the rear.

A couple of hard-nosed prospectors who'd given Asha her rough initiation a few days ago now cowered in fear when they saw her holding the derringer.

When Brett reached the alley door, he stood aside, guns still levelled as the Cheyenne maidens filed past him.

'The first man to poke his head outside is buzzard bait,' Brett warned.

He backed outside himself and untied his roan while the apprehensive Indian maidens gathered around Chameli in the darkness of the alley. Relieved to be out of that hellhole, they were still shaking in fear.

'How will we get out of white man's town?' Chameli asked.

'See those two Lazy F horses?'

'One belongs to the evil snake, De Heus,' Chameli indicated the chestnut. 'The other is Josh's horse.'

Brett said, 'I'll keep watch on the saloon while you and Asha fetch them.'

They didn't ask any questions. Instead, they simply complied and ran to the branded horses while Brett stood with his two guns aimed at the saloon doorway. The gunfighter saw shadows moving inside, heard the low buzz of urgent conversation. It wouldn't be long before someone took a chance and ventured out.

Chameli and Asha untethered the horses from their tie-rail.

'Come with me,' Brett told them, 'all of you.'

Brett walked his roan to the hanging sign, with Chameli and Asha leading the two mounts they'd untethered. The other Cheyenne girls were at their heels. At the head of the alley, Brett held up his hand, motioning them to gather around him as he checked the muddy street. The two hairy prospectors who'd been punching each other a few minutes ago now sat drinking coffee amicably outside the Two Jacks Card House. The same drunken miners he'd seen when he rode in were still sleeping it off on the hard wooden boardwalks. More importantly, the ageing whore on the wagon was still displaying her wares and the mule stood like it was frozen.

Brett led the way alongside the board-walk.

Still no one challenged them. Maybe the townsfolk were mostly asleep. Speaking softly, Brett warned the girls to keep close to him. He turned to Chameli and Asha, reminding them to keep their eyes peeled and their guns ready.

Then he began to walk his horse across the muddy main street.

They were half way over when one of the prospectors out front of the Two Jacks bellowed out, 'What the hell's going on?'

Suddenly, faces pressed against windows, doors whined open and a customer emerged from Kate's Cats brothel yanking up his trousers. Moments later, prospectors ventured out of the Painted Woman Shebang and Wildcat Camp sprang to life. Lamps were lit all over town. The wrinkled harlot on the wagon stared in bewilderment as Brett Cassidy and eight Indian girls loomed out of the darkness. Brett's boots squelched in the deep mud as he led the roan right up to her.

'Sorry, ma'am, we need your wagon,' he said tersely. 'So get down unless you want a free ride to Cheyenne Territory.'

'This wagon belongs to my boss!' she wailed.

Ignoring the screeching woman, Brett spoke in Cheyenne to the girls. 'Unhitch the mule and back your horses into harness.'

By now the Painted Woman patrons, furious their girls had been snatched from under their very noses, appeared at the head of their alley. Brett fired a single shot that tore through the hanging sign and sent them scattering. Then he saw shadowy figures outside the old law office. Two bullets thudding into the wall warned three inebriated miners he meant business and they went scurrying, one falling into a water trough in his haste to escape Brett's slugs. By now Asha had the mule out of its harness and at Brett's command the Indian girls dragged the old Kate's Cat off the wagon. She lashed out at them, then tripped and fell sprawling into the mud. The Painted Woman's patrons returned and this time their slugs peppered the side of the rocking wagon.

Brett felt the hot breath of a bullet flying inches from his face. He didn't want to kill any innocent townsfolk but he emptied both guns, his bullets scarring walls and ripping the big sign to shreds. As a consequence, most of the irate miners once more fled for cover and dozens of doors were slammed shut.

But Brett figured the respite would be brief.

He was an unwanted stranger and the patrons of Delaney's saloon were aroused and angry. Some folks living in Wildcat Camp wouldn't give a damn about the loss of a few Indian girls, but others, particularly those who frequented the Painted Woman, were infuriated. This crazy stranger was stealing their property!

Darkness was Brett's friend.

He reloaded his guns as Chameli and Asha harnessed the two horses to the wagon. The screaming whore, plastered with sticky black mud, finally retreated to the boardwalk and ran into Kate's Cats brothel. Brett ordered all the Cheyenne maidens to climb in to the wagon. They all scrambled on board and at Brett's command the eldest squaw, who'd been captured at the fishing traps, slid on to the driving seat and grabbed the reins.

'We're moving out,' Brett announced. 'I'll ride ahead. Chameli and Asha, you stake out in the back of the wagon.'

Brett swung into the saddle. He leaned over and released the wagon brake. Wasting no time, he nudged the roan into a steady walk as he began to escort the cumbersome wagon through the clammy mud. Looking back over the street, Asha glimpsed the youngest of the two prospectors who'd so brutally initiated her. She despised him. She only had a derringer, but spurred by bitter hatred, she couldn't resist pointing it at him and pulling the trigger. There was but one shot in her handgun and the bullet bored into the man's upper left thigh. He buckled at the knees, crashed to the boardwalk and lay yelling for help.

Riding ahead of the lumbering wagon, Brett reached the lamplight thrown by three saloons. None of these were owned by Delaney and they all had their resident, well-paid saloon girls. These girls actually cheered as they watched their Cheyenne opposition being taken out of town. It meant more customers for them. However, a few irate regulars who frequented the Painted Woman Shebang still persisted in chasing Brett and the Cheyenne girls. A couple of rifle bullets thudded into the rear of the escaping wagon. Other shots fired by prospectors who'd drunk too much and should be asleep in their quarters winged wide. One shattered the barber's window. Another killed a pigeon on the roof of the only chapel in Wildcat Camp. Despite the inebriated condition of the mob swarming behind the wagon as it swayed past the undertaker's, Brett decided to take no chances. One of their bullets might just find its target so he lifted his rifle from its scabbard, turned in the saddle and fired. Six rifle bullets, one by one, ploughed into the mud at their feet, scattering them once again, all except one stout miner, who practically lived in the Painted Woman Shebang. He was puffing and blowing as he ran up the street chasing the escaping wagon. He loomed closer and when one of the maidens in the wagon screamed a timely warning, Chameli levelled the gun Brett had given her and fired. Her first shot was wide of her target, smashing the undertaker's window. The second tore splinters from the boardwalk on the other side of the street, but when she fired again, her bullet was so close to the charging miner that it kicked mud into his face. He fled like a frightened rabbit.

Brett urged his roan into a lope as they reached town limits.

A couple more bullets were fired along main street but they winged well wide as the wagon swayed out of the lamp light into the night. The town fell silent. The men of Wildcat Camp who weren't sensibly home in their beds at this hour gathered on the main street. Few were sober and they certainly resented these girls being snatched away from them, but most of them now conceded the Cheyenne maidens had proved to be disappointing. They didn't have the passion and expertise of Kate's Cats or any other 'soiled doves' in town. And anyway, Mr Delaney would find replacements. He always did. Aside from that consideration, pursuing the Indian girls would be risky out there in the darkness and these men of Wildcat Camp decided it was preferable to go back to their respective watering holes and have another drink — or two.

Unchallenged now, Brett rode ahead of the rolling wagon.

One hour out of Wildcat Camp, they left the main trail and took the thin track that forked towards Cheyenne Territory.

★ ★ ★

With De Heus about to be measured for a coffin by the Wildcat Camp's frowning, cigar-smoking undertaker, most of the Painted Woman's patrons had gone back to their tents and cabins. Their host was dead, their girls had been snatched from under their very noses, so they might as well be getting some shut-eye. Only a handful remained to help themselves to free rotgut, including the old prospector who was still fuming at having been denied his time with Asha.

This old timer rambled down to the river with a wooden bucket and scooped some water. The town was at last going to sleep as he stumbled back with the bucket and unceremoniously tipped the icy contents over Josh's sprawled body.

Josh quivered, moaned, then clutched air as the freezing deluge jerked him back from unconsciousness. Swearing, spitting blood, he sat up, drenched to the skin.

'What — what the hell's going on, Henry?'

'That crazy stranger whipped you with

his gun.'

'Bastard!' Josh exploded.

Henry elaborated, 'Stole the gals, all of them, then killed Anton. Shot him down like a dog in front of everyone.' Josh stared at Henry, one of the many regulars in the Painted Woman Shebang. Muttering, he climbed unsteadily to his feet as the old prospector recalled what had happened.

'You all let him just walk out of here?' Josh asked incredulously.

'He had the drop on us and he gave my gun — and yours — to the Injun gals. I was flat to this floor, but by all accounts, he just marched out with them. No one dared to slap leather, me included. They took Anton's horse, and yours, and packed the gals into one of Mr Delaney's wagons.'

'Who was this loon?'

'No one knows,' Henry said helplessly.

'Except me,' the undertaker called out.

Josh staggered across the brothel, then through the open door into the saloon where the town undertaker, Luther Lewis, had heard their conversation while just completing his careful measurement of the deceased. He prided himself on saving money by making his caskets the exact size needed.

'You know who that stranger was?' Josh asked hoarsely.

'My father, bless his departed soul, once had a mortician's parlour in Lincoln City,' Lewis said eloquently. 'That's where I learned the blessed trade of helping people in their grief and sorrow.'

'Quit the sales talk, Lewis,' Josh snapped. 'Just tell me what you know about this stranger.'

'He's a professional gunfighter, name of Mr Brett Cassidy,' Lewis told him. 'Killed a former lawman who was a disgrace to his badge. My father gave me the job of measuring the evil man.' He smiled. 'It was my first time.'

'You sure about the name?'

'Very sure, sir,' Luther Lewis confirmed. 'One of those escaping Indian women put a bullet through my front window. When I ran into my parlour and looked out on the street, I saw him plainly in the light thrown by Kate's — uh — establishment. It was definitely him, Mr Brett Cassidy, professional hired gun.' He shook his head. 'I have no idea what he would be doing here.'

'He came here for one obvious reason,' Josh growled.

'To steal our Cheyenne gals,' Henry supplied.

'To steal Mr *Delaney's gals*,' Josh corrected the oldster. 'He owns this saloon and everyone and everything in it.'

'Yes, of course,' Henry agreed.

'I'm sure Mr Delaney would want to know who this murdering thief is,' Josh told them both. 'I'll ride to Red Butte now. In the meantime, Henry, I'm putting you in charge.'

'Uh, me?' Henry gulped.

'Yeah, you know the rotgut prices. If customers want a gal, they'll have to wait. I'm sure Mr Delaney will find a couple for me to bring back.'

'I'll do my best, Josh.'

'Ah, a promotion, Henry,' the undertaker congratulated the old prospector. 'Not quite the same as the late Mr De Heus, who has been promoted to Glory. Now can I prevail upon you to help me carry Mr De Heus back to my chapel?'

Josh strode out of the Painted Woman. With his horse gone, he made his way to Delaney's Freight Line. There would be saddles and horses there in the livery. He aimed to be out of town in ten minutes and be in Red Butte soon after sun-up. With Anton De Heus under the clay, maybe Mr Delaney would promote him to manager of the Painted Woman Shebang.

He rubbed his hands together in anticipation.

12

I'll do any that, josh.

On a mounting admiringly, the under-
...ker congratulation n... and protector.
...ot quite the same as the late Mr. De

Garth Delaney rose early, brewed coffee on his new Philadelphian cast iron potbelly stove and waited on his front verandah. Built on the hillock that shadowed Red Butte, his new stone house overlooked the town and its streets. His many enterprises were all profitable; he had so much money in the town bank that its manager almost licked his boots when he walked in the front door. His personal fortune had almost doubled in the last two years. After all, he had an empire. The freight line was raking in money and his ranches carried thousands of beeves. Once he was able to run his stock on that settler land in Lonesome Valley, he would truly be a cattle king. His saloons, especially the Last Chance in Red Butte, were making him richer by the day.

Then of course, there were his latest businesses in Wildcat Camp.

Yet Garth Delaney wanted more.

He was a greedy man, never satisfied.

Yet even though he virtually had all he needed, there was no Mrs Delaney. Sure, he could have Jessie and almost any other saloon woman he wanted, but Delaney figured a man of his wealth should be able to marry someone more suitable. Maybe the mayor's comely daughter? Or a high society woman from New Orleans? Perhaps a mail order bride from the east? He could certainly afford the very best woman in the country and, once he'd settled the Lonesome Valley problem, he'd pay more attention to his personal needs.

A glimmer of light signified dawn was breaking.

He sipped his coffee, waiting impatiently.

Ten minutes later a lone rider left town limits and latched on to the dusty trail that climbed to Delaney's elevated home. Watching, Delaney frowned as the rider came closer. He was expecting two men. Something was wrong. He stood up as Buff Malloy emptied his saddle.

'Where's Cassidy?' Delaney demanded.

'He's gone,' Malloy said simply.

'What do you mean?'

'Like I said, gone, Mr Delaney,' Buff Malloy said. 'Knocked on Jessie's door just to remind him of his duty. She answered the door. She'd obviously been out of it and stank of wine and mumbled something about he must have gone in the middle of the night. When she woke up, which was just before I arrived, her window was open. Figured he slipped out the back. Anyway, I checked the livery and sure enough, his roan horse was missing. I reckon the bird has flown, Mr Delaney.'

'I gave him Jessie for the night as a signing-on gift,' Delaney fumed. 'Double-crossing bastard!'

'I don't think he even took advantage of your gift, Mr Delaney,' Malloy said. 'When I called, Jessie looked like she'd slept in her saloon dress.'

'Makes him ungrateful too,' Delaney said.

'He's probably riding home by now.'

'All trails cross, Buff,' Delaney reminded him. 'Might take a while, but we'll see him again.'

'And the Kid will want to be there,' Malloy said. 'He owes him.'

Delaney drank the last dregs of his coffee. 'Anyway, forget about Cassidy for now. The job we talked about and planned for Cassidy to execute is now yours.'

'Figured as much, Mr Delaney,' Buff Malloy said.

'Take one of the Lazy F boys with you.'

'Grogan's still in town. Saw him sleeping in the livery.'

'Wake him up and do what needs to be done.'

'Sure, Mr Delaney.'

'You're a loyal man, Buff,' Delaney praised Malloy as he remounted his brown gelding. 'Expect some extra pay this month.'

Buff Malloy rode down the track back into Red Butte.

Grogan was just awake, sitting

hunched in the hay when Malloy strode into the livery stable.

'Get some grub, saddle up and come with me,' Malloy told him.

The new day's dazzling sun was clear of the eastern rims and Red Butte was stirring to life as the two men rode out. They headed past the stock yards and took the trail that swung past Red Butte's fenced cemetery before turning into Lonesome Valley. First they rode by Delaney's Lazy F ranch and then continued going further up the valley where settlers had fenced off open range.

Here they left the trail, instead keeping to timber cover as they drifted past the first sodbuster acreage. They saw a new settler and his buxom young wife struggling to brand a calf. Malloy figured the man would have made a perfect target but Delaney had someone else in mind.

As they rode, he recalled that other killing.

Together with Grogan and two other Lazy F riders, they'd trapped outspoken settler Tom McBeath at gunpoint on a cliff top. They never fired a shot, instead hurling him over the cliff to his death below. McBeath had left behind a pretty wife. More than once Malloy had been tempted to ride over and call on his widow. After all, Harmony McBeath had no idea he'd taken part in the cold-blooded murder of her husband. It was an accident, the coroner had declared. Malloy grinned as he remembered taking Mr Delaney's two hundred dollars bribe over to Coroner Leonard Makepeace's place ten minutes before he left for the court hearing.

They were adjacent to Harmony's spread now and Malloy slowed his gelding as he saw the widow milking the solitary cow she owned. She was indeed a fine-looking woman and she must be missing what a man could give her. Yes, maybe he should call, whether she was willing or not, but not now because he had business to take care of, business with her neighbour. So he wrenched his mind off Widow McBeath and rode ahead of Grogan to a clump of large, smooth boulders overlooking the trail that followed Will Quade's fence.

Leaving their horses tied to an arrowhead pine, Malloy and Grogan climbed to the boulder crest.

It was the perfect stakeout.

Here, high above the trail, they could see the whole one hundred and sixty acres being farmed by Will and Amanda Quade. Lately, Delaney had been particularly irked by Quade. Despite his advancing years, Quade had become the unelected leader of the Lonesome Valley homesteaders and Delaney had heard that meetings uniting the settlers had been held regularly in his big hay barn. Now, Delaney had decreed, Will Quade must be eliminated.

Holding his Smithfield rifle, Malloy lay flat between two boulders.

Next to him, Grogan crouched alongside a mossy boulder. He carried a long hunting rifle.

The acreage stretching below them was undulating grassland dotted with sheep and timber. A log cabin dwarfed by the barn had smoke curling languidly from its blackened stone chimney. Two dogs roamed the front verandah. Alongside the cabin was a small vegetable garden. The Quades were obviously both inside, but the two men staked out in the boulders would wait all day if necessary. In actual fact, they only had to wait half an hour before Will Quade opened the cabin door and began to stroll towards his barn.

Malloy lifted his rifle and squinted down its barrel.

He drew a careful bead on the old settler, aiming at his chest.

Waiting till Quade made the barn, Malloy squeezed his trigger. The Springfield boomed and recoiled against his shoulder. With the gunshot echoing out over Lonesome Valley, Quade slumped against the barn wall. Blood blotched his shirt but he managed to keep his feet as his wife came screaming out of their cabin.

'Reckon you just winged him, Buff.'

Malloy fired a second shot that splintered into the barn inches from his head. Then Grogan flicked ash from his cigarette tip and fired his hunting rifle. It was Grogan's shot that finally snuffed out the old homesteader's life. Quade pitched headlong to the ground where his weeping wife threw herself over him. Just as Malloy and Grogan began to retreat to their horses, they heard Amanda's poignant cry ring out over the valley. 'You filthy yeller sons-of-bitches!'

'Want me to take the woman too?' Grogan asked. He patted his rifle and boasted, 'Just one shot would shut her up forever. It'd be a real pleasure.'

'No, leave her,' Buff Malloy said. 'Let's just get out of here.'

'You're the boss,' Grogan said, shrugging off his disappointment.

They reached their horses and mounted.

Keeping to timber cover, they headed back down-valley.

Half a dozen settlers who'd heard rifle fire and the woman's high-pitched screaming were already riding the trail below them and Malloy motioned the Lazy F man to rein his horse behind a large wild dewberry bush as their dust rolled past.

When the coast was finally clear, they took the passage that led through to Rattler Canyon where they joined the trail for Red Butte.

It was closing in on high noon when they rode into the town and made straight for the Last Chance Saloon.

Entering, they saw Delaney standing by the bar counter.

Immediately, Malloy figured something was wrong, seriously wrong. Although he was aware that Garth Delaney had a Colt revolver in a shoulder holster concealed under his suit coat, he was now wearing a gun belt strapped around his waist. A second gun nestled in its right-side leather. Apart from his conspicuous weaponry, Delaney's face had changed into a mask of angry hostility. Kid Jorgenson, his arm still in its sling, stood scowling beside his boss.

'Job's done,' Malloy announced quietly.

'Yeah,' Grogan chimed in, 'Quade's ready for Boothill.'

But there was no compliment from Delaney.

Instead, he declared bluntly, 'We've been betrayed.'

Malloy and Grogan stared at their boss.

'What do you mean, Mr Delaney?' the Lazy F man asked.

Delaney cocked a thumb at the man drinking alone under the balcony.

It was Josh, bruised and exhausted, here from Wildcat Camp.

Delaney spoke in low tones, 'Josh just rode in with some bad news concerning Brett Cassidy. First I thought Cassidy had just decided to turn his back on our deal and ride home, wherever that is, but it seems I made a damn fool mistake. He's a snake-in-the-grass!'

'Told you all that Cassidy was trouble,' Jorgenson said, smirking, unable to hide his satisfaction at being proved right.

Delaney snapped, 'Button up, Kid.'

'Yeah, sure, Mr Delaney,' Jorgenson said, his grin fading.

Delaney resumed, 'Last night he snuck out of Jessie's room, but he didn't just vamoose. He rode to Wildcat Camp.'

'Whatever for?'

'For the crazy purpose of stealing my Cheyenne gals.'

'Hell's fires!' Malloy croaked.

'Apparently Cassidy said he was taking the girls home where they belong,' Delaney quoted what Josh had been told when he came to.

'You mean, Cheyenne Territory?'

'Cassidy busted them out of my Painted Woman Shebang.'

Malloy was incredulous. 'What! Singlehanded?'

'From what Josh said, yes, and in doing so, shot and killed our good friend, Anton De Heus,' Delaney told them.

'Anton dead!' Malloy exploded, his cheeks reddening in anger.

'Being buried today.'

'There's only one possible reason why

Cassidy would ride all the way to Wildcat Camp, steal those gals and double-cross us,' Garth Delaney said grimly. 'He has to be working for those bloody home-steaders and part of his job must be to take those gals back to their Cheyenne villages to stop the Injun raids on Lone-some Valley.'

'In other words, Cassidy is a turncoat,' Jorgenson said.

'But Cassidy's a professional gun-fighter,' Malloy protested, frowning. 'How could that bunch of lousy pen-ny-pinching sodbusters afford to pay him more than you? Doesn't make sense to me.'

'I don't know how he came to work for them, but he must be on their pay-roll,' Delaney replied. 'Right now he's probably arrived in Cheyenne Territory smoking a peace pipe after returning those gals to their menfolk. That might stop the Injuns going on the warpath against the Lonesome Valley settlers, but it won't stop Cassidy getting what's coming to him when next he shows his face.'

'If he dares to show his face,' Malloy said.

'Maybe he'll just return those women and keep riding,' Grogan suggested.

'A man like Cassidy wouldn't do that,' Delaney predicted. 'He's been hired by those homesteaders but he's only earned half his pay. That means we'll be in his sights for sure.'

The bartender served drinks for them all.

'However, we'll be ready for him,' Delaney added confidently.

'I can't imagine him actually riding into Red Butte,' Malloy said.

'I agree with Buff,' Grogan said, becoming decidedly uneasy.

'A man who'd walk into a brothel and take out eight Injun whores would ride in anywhere. He'll come, sure enough. And when he does show his face in town, we'll be ready for him,' Delaney told them. 'As you can see, Josh isn't up to it. I'm sending him back to Wildcat Camp, so we'll need to get ourselves some insurance. Grogan, finish your drink, then ride straight to the Lazy F and bring back a couple of hardcases.'

Grogan didn't need to consider for long. 'I suggest Parker and the Mex. There are stories about Parker. He definitely killed a man in Californy. Some say he shot him in the back and the law's after him. As for the Mex, well, everyone knows he's just plain mean, very handy with a gun or knife.'

'Fetch both men,' Delaney told him. 'Bring them here cold, hard and sober.'

'Sure, Mr Delaney,' Grogan agreed, gulping down the last of his whiskey.

Waiting until Grogan left through the batwings, Delaney turned to Malloy and Jorgenson. 'We need to make plans. Come to my office.'

* * *

Brett Cassidy had escorted the Cheyenne girls all safely back to their camp where he was thanked by Leaning Bear and the tribal elders. No more war smoke would rise. They would live at peace with the white settlers. It was Leaning Bear himself who escorted Brett out of Indian Country.

The gunfighter was in the saddle all day.

Now he came out of the dusk as the sad, subdued singing of the poignant hymn 'Shall We Gather at the River' rose above the cemetery, disturbing the evening stillness. He rode slowly, almost at the end of his long trail out of Cheyenne Territory. He'd been headed for Red Butte but the weeping and the motionless shadows around graves made the gunfighter draw rein and sit saddle. Preacher O'Toole was conducting the funeral service, now reading the prayers slowly and carefully. Brett ran his eyes over the mourners. Most of them weren't smartly dressed like most townsfolk would be. Then his eyes came to rest on Harmony McBeath standing next to the widow. Like most other women, Harmony wore a black hat and dress.

He figured these folks had to be homesteaders.

Reverend O'Toole raised his voice and said the name of the man he was burying. That name echoed out over the graveyard. It was William Quade.

Brett nudged his roan closer, right to the very edge of the mourners.

'William Augustus Quade was a good, decent, hardworking man, the very salt of the earth,' Preacher O'Toole praised the deceased man. His voice began to break. 'He didn't deserve to be gunned down by someone skulking in the rocks like a lowdown, cowardly coyote.'

The mourners murmured their approval at the preacher's graphic summation of the crime. They were angry, but Brett Cassidy also saw the fear on their faces. Their leader had been murdered. Who would be next? Brett wouldn't need to ask anyone who they thought had given the order to kill an old man like Quade. They knew the answer; so did he. Still in the saddle, Brett Cassidy looked down at Red Butte. Lights were being lit all over the town. Doubtless Delaney and his crew were down there now, probably gloating over the murder of another homesteader. He felt anger mounting inside him — not hot anger, but cold and calculating.

He knew what he had to do.

Preacher O'Toole's graveside homily was drawing to its close.

Brett heard Widow Quade's loud weeping and watched as Harmony placed a comforting arm around her shoulder now the time had come for the final committal. Four sturdy homesteaders used two ropes to lower the pine box into the grave.

'Ashes to ashes, dust to dust . . .'

Preacher Jason O'Toole recited the words he'd read out many times, far too many times, since coming to Red Butte.

Now he was closer, Brett looked over the mourners again. He recognised Mrs Tully who was throwing a handful of dust over the receding coffin. It was then Brett saw another shadowy rider on the far side of the graveyard, someone who'd been watching proceedings without being part of the funeral. He was in the saddle, a stout, middle-aged man with a black moustache curling over his crooked teeth and fat lips. He wasn't dressed in mourning clothes, but wore a stained apron over his red check shirt and creased black pants. Brett had seen the silent watcher before.

He was the bartender in Delaney's Last Chance Saloon.

And this rider had glimpsed Brett too.

Even before Quade's casket crunched the clay at the bottom of the grave, the bartender hastily backed his grey gelding and rode swiftly away into the ghostly twilight. Brett had no doubt where he was headed.

Within minutes Delaney would hear his news that the gunfighter was back.

The mourners paid their last respects, then thanked Preacher O'Toole and shook his hand. Just as O'Toole slipped his prayer book into a shoulder bag and made ready to leave, Brett saw his wife Tabitha. She caught sight of him too and clutched her man's arm. It was as if she knew there was going to be killing and she was scared. Brett nodded to her before she hustled her preacher husband back to their horse and buggy. Two of the homesteaders began shovelling dirt to fill the grave; others were standing back, silent and tearful. Mrs Quade went to join them. Harmony was about to do the same when she glimpsed the tall gunfighter motionless, starkly etched against the setting sun.

'Brett!' she exclaimed, hastening from the grave.

The gunfighter dismounted as she reached him. 'Just rode in.'

'They murdered Will in cold blood,' Harmony blurted out. 'Gunshots rang out over the valley, some of the men went over and found tracks that led back to town. We all know who sent those men!'

'Sorry about Will, he was a good man,' Brett said gently.

'More than just a good man,' Harmony said. 'Will Quade was the heart and soul of this valley.' She nodded to the forlorn group of mourners lingering in the dusk. 'Now these folks are talking about leaving their spreads and moving on.' She turned from looking at them and said hastily, 'No one's blaming you that Will died. Will had told us you'd gone on a mission on our behalf, to find those Cheyenne girls and return them to their villages so there wouldn't be any more Indian raids.'

'The girls are home and the chief assured me you settlers won't be raided,' Brett told her. 'There's just one last thing I need to do.'

Brett looked past the cemetery to the lights of Red Butte.

'You'll have no one to help you,' Harmony reminded him.

'Not looking for help,' he said.

Harmony whispered, 'Please be careful, Brett Cassidy, and I'm saying that for a reason.'

Their eyes met in the dying light as her hand brushed his. Then, impulsively, Harmony reached up, cupped his face with her trembling hands and pressed her soft lips to his. It was a quick kiss which he returned for a few fleeting moments before she stepped back from him. She was suddenly aware that the other homesteaders had seen what had happened between them but she didn't care.

'That's the reason, Brett,' she said as he climbed back into the saddle.

'Ride home with the others, Harmony,' he advised, adding softly, 'I'll be back later.'

'I pray you will,' Harmony murmured fervently.

Brett gathered up his reins.

He took a last look at the men filling Will's grave where his widow wept and watched the dirt hitting the coffin, then he glanced at the homesteaders huddled together under two tall spruce trees.

Finally, he looked at Harmony and saw the light of hope in her eyes.

The gunfighter nudged his roan into a walk and headed for Red Butte.

13

The last glow of sundown faded into the gathering darkness and a sudden chill wind whispered like a ghost from the distant mountains as Brett Cassidy reached the edge of Red Butte. Lamps were being lit all over town, mostly in homes, very few along First Street where just half a dozen lanterns hung under boardwalk verandahs. The gunfighter faced a street of dark shadows and even darker alleys. He rode slowly, one hand resting on his right side gun.

He drew adjacent to the preacher's parsonage. Jason and Tabitha O'Toole had just arrived home minutes ago and they hadn't as yet lit an inside lamp. But they were there at their front window, watching him ride by.

Then Tabitha drew the curtains sharply across.

Brett rode by the Tabernacle Chapel, then the Quaker Meeting House.

An owl hooted from the old loft behind the blacksmith's forge. Smoke still wisped from the forge but, like most other townsfolk, the blacksmith was nowhere to be seen.

The lamp hanging from a hook outside the Black Deuce Card House cast a faint red light over its open door. Brett heard no sound from inside but cigarette smoke hung in the open doorway. This was a Delaney enterprise so Brett was doubly wary as he rode by. The law office was shut, in complete darkness. He figured that both badge-wearers would be safely home. He rode further down the street. The bartender would have alerted Delaney by now, so he could be facing a stacked deck, but he'd faced others in the past and lived.

But this would definitely be the last time.

This was to repay a debt.

By now he was close to the Last Chance Saloon.

Usually it was well lit, but a solitary lamp glowed under its verandah. Its windows were clogged with dust but he could just glimpse another single lamp through the glass pane. Then he heard the soft tinkle of the piano but nothing else, no conversation, no clink of glasses, just silence. He drew adjacent to Delaney's Freight Line Office. It was wreathed in darkness. So was the Red Butte Lodging House that was almost opposite the saloon. He glimpsed movement in the lodging house foyer. It was dark, like nearly every other building on First Street, but someone was there.

'Mr Cassidy! Mr Cassidy!' came the urgent summons from Widow Tully who was hidden in the darkness. The resentment at Delaney for short-changing her rose to its crescendo. She whispered, 'Man with rifle staked out in here! Third window!'

'Thank you, ma'am,' Brett said softly.

The gunfighter slid noiselessly from his horse and slipped inside past Ma Tully who was still wrestling with the enormity of what she'd just done. He strode to the passage door and walked to

Room Three. Slowly, carefully, he turned the big brass handle and eased the door open to a thin slit. He saw a burly figure of a man crouched with his long rifle beside the open window. If Brett had ridden a few more feet, he would have been blasted out of the saddle. Using his boot, Brett edged the door open wider. The would-be ambusher still hadn't heard him. Stealthy as an Indian scout, Brett approached him and finally thrust a Colt Peacemaker into his spine.

'You have a choice,' the gunfighter said slowly. 'Either you can be a damn fool and sing out, in which case I'll blow you apart, or you can talk and I'll merely put you asleep. When you wake up, you'll have a sore head but you'll still be breathing. Decide now.'

'I do not wish to die, *señor*,' the Mexican implored.

'You're working for Delaney,' Brett accused.

The Mexican sweated. '*Sí, sí*, my very big mistake, *señor*.'

'They're in the saloon?'

'*Sí.*'

'How many?'

'Five of them.'

'Where are they staked out?'

'Señor Delaney will kill me!'

'And I will if you don't talk now,' Brett warned. 'Where the hell are they?'

'Señores Grogan and Parker are high up, on balcony,' the Mexican whimpered. 'The one they call 'Kid' is behind bar, but I think he has no gun. Señor Malloy is at poker table by balcony stairs.' He was weeping in fear as he now came to betray his boss. 'And Señor Delaney, he is in office doorway.' He shook visibly. 'Be smart, *amigo*, there are too many guns against you. Ride out before you get killed!'

Brett brought his gun handle down on the Mexican's skull and the hapless man crumbled like stale cake and slumped to the shredded carpet on Room Three's floor.

The gunfighter looked out the open window at the street. No one moved there. He backed to the passageway and saw Mrs Tully wringing her hands in the foyer.

'One more favour, ma'am.'

'Name it,' she trembled.

'Look after my horse.'

'Yes, certainly, Mr Cassidy.'

'I'll see you soon,' he promised.

'I pray so,' Ma Tully said fervently.

The gunfighter walked back to the street and appraised the Last Chance Saloon. The piano music had faded away. He heard an angry expletive from Jessie followed by the slamming of a door. Obviously there had been a disagreement inside. But then all became as silent as an Indian burial ground. He saw that none of the four windows had been cleaned, all being caked with dust and grime. Unless someone inside stood at the batwings, it was unlikely he could be detected crossing the street.

He lifted his six-shooters.

It was time for justice, time for his guns to speak.

Half way across First Street, he halted and levelled one gun at the furthest right window. He fired a single bullet that bored a hole through the top of the dusty pane. Immediately the Last Chance Saloon erupted with the thunder of guns, all instinctively aimed in the direction where the sound of the explosion came from.

Bullets hammered and shattered windows into a thousand fragments, exposing the street, but the gunfighter wasn't there to be seen. Instead, taking advantage of their attention being momentarily diverted, he barged in through the batwings, both guns blazing.

The Mexican cowpoke had told the truth.

Grogan and Parker were crouched on the elevated balcony, emptying their guns at the smashed window. Malloy saw the gunfighter and shouted a desperate warning.

But it was too late.

Brett's first bullet thudded into Grogan's chest. Bellowing like a stricken steer, Grogan grabbed the balcony rail, lost his grip and plummeted headlong to the faro table below. His heavy body split the table in two before slithering to the floor. Parker managed to fire one hasty shot that splintered the batwings inches from Brett's shoulder, but before he could pull trigger again, the gunfighter's twin Colts boomed in deadly unison.

Dead on his feet, Parker crashed to the balcony carpet and lay as still as stone.

Brett Cassidy turned to face the bar. Kid Jorgenson had one arm in his sling, the other resting on the bar counter next to his beer. Just a couple of paces away, Malloy tipped a poker table on to its side, spilling cards and drinks into the sawdust, then crouched behind it. Still standing just inside the creaking batwings, Brett blasted two slugs into the table top. The upturned table shuddered and a third bullet bored right through, just nicking Malloy's shoulder. Cursing, Buff Malloy reared to his feet and began pumping lead at Brett Cassidy who stood like Nemesis, motionless in the eerie half light. Two of Malloy's bullets burned past Brett's ribs and a third tore flesh from the gunfighter's left arm. Ignoring the stabbing pain, Brett fired a single bullet that lifted Malloy clean off his feet and slammed him hard against the bar. Brett's next shot snuffed out Malloy's life before he hit the floor.

Jorgenson cried out, 'Don't shoot me! I'm unarmed, as you can see!'

Suddenly Brett heard a scuffle and Jessie's door was booted open.

Using Jessie as a human shield, Delaney had his left arm clamped around her waist, his right hand holding his derringer to the side of her head. The saloon girl was white-faced, frozen in terror as he pushed her roughly out of her room.

'I know you two go back a long way, Cassidy,' Delaney said. 'Well, unless you want to see your old friend's face blown off, drop your guns!'

'He means it, Brett,' Jessie wailed.

'I'm sure he does,' Brett said coldly.

The gunfighter's eyes were like dark pools of death as he slowly lowered his Peacemakers. He didn't drop them, he just slipped them both back into their leather holsters. Kid Jorgenson chuckled, then he laughed mockingly as his hand that had been resting on the wooden counter now slid into his sling and pulled out the six-shooter he'd had concealed there.

'I'll take him, boss,' Jorgenson boasted. 'It'll be my pleasure.'

He angled his gun to aim at Brett but before he could pull the trigger, the shadow of a man loomed at the shattered window. A long carbine held by the Reverend Jason O'Toole intruded into the saloon. A split second later, the gun thundered and a bullet carved into Jorgenson's ribcage, killing him instantly. The Kid dropped, his gun clattering over the bar top. Momentarily, Delaney's attention switched from Brett and focused on the preacher at the window. Jessie took advantage of this brief respite, wriggled free from her boss and scrambled to one side.

Suddenly it was just Brett Cassidy and Garth Delaney facing each other across the dimly-lit Last Chance Saloon. Brett's draw was a blur, his right side gun clearing leather as Delaney levelled his derringer. Without seeming to aim, Brett fired from his hip, his gun blasting a slug into Delaney's chest as the saloon owner's finger found the trigger. Delaney's derringer snarled as he staggered to his left side, his bullet winging well wide of the gunfighter who calmly fired the final shot to finish him off. Brett turned to the man at the broken window.

'Thanks, Preach,' Brett said. 'I owe you.'

'Maybe it's the best sermon I've preached for a while,' O'Toole said, still shaking visibly. 'My wife didn't want me to come — but I had to.'

'Reckon there's one more thing you can do for me,' Brett Cassidy said. He nodded to where Jessie was sobbing into her hands. 'This lady's special to me. Right now she needs some pastoral care.' He added wryly, 'And maybe some preaching wouldn't go astray either if she's in the mood to listen.'

'Yes, yes of course,' Jason O'Toole agreed.

While the preacher tramped the boardwalk to come in through the batwings, Brett walked through the now-silent saloon and entered Delaney's office. He went straight to the saloon owner's desk. What he was looking for was still on top of Delaney's pile of papers. Selecting two documents, he folded them and strode back through the saloon and outside. The street was no longer deserted. Half a dozen folks had ventured out on to the boardwalks and two more lamps had been lit. It was like the town was coming to life, new life. He made straight for the lodging house where Ma Tully regarded him with awe. She was trembling, drinking the strongest coffee she'd brewed for years.

'So you sold this place to Delaney?'

'Yes,' she repeated what she'd told him yesterday.

The gunfighter took the folded documents from his shirt pocket. Wide-eyed, Ma Tully gasped as he ripped the bill of sale into pieces, but handed the original title deed of the Red Butte Lodging House back to her.

'I don't believe you ever sold it to him, ma'am,' Brett Cassidy said, shrugging.

'Mr Delaney!' she exclaimed. 'Thank you!'

He asked her, 'My horse?'

'Safely stabled behind the Lodging House,' she told him.

'So long, Ma Tully.'

Two minutes later Brett Cassidy rode his horse back up First Street. Behind him, the local undertaker and his assistant were running like rabbits to join the townsfolk now venturing into the Last Chance Saloon. Dozens more lamps were being lit. In fact, as Brett rode out, it seemed like the only unlit place on First Street was the law office. Brett had a hunch both lawmen would be replaced tomorrow.

He rode his roan right out of town and headed for Lonesome Valley.

★ ★ ★

Riding under the canopy of a big full moon and a million stars, Brett Cassidy reached the long valley where settlers had made their homes. With Delaney in a pine box, the homesteaders would be able to farm their land and bring up their families in peace. As for Brett, he hoped this really was his last mission as a professional gunfighter. Of course, he'd put away his guns and 'settled down' once before but he wanted to give it another try. This time he had a very special reason. Well, he hoped he had.

He reached Harmony's fence line and found the gate she'd left open for him.

Riding through, he closed the gate behind him and followed the track across the dark grass to where Harmony's lamp flickered in her single window. It was as if that light was beckoning him. He passed the old wagon and the barn. Harmony had heard his approach because she flung open the door and stood there waiting. The young widow had changed out of her mourning garb into a blue floral dress she'd made for herself. Even as Brett rode in, he could make out her wide-open eyes, glowing face and the deliciously firm curves her dress could not conceal.

He reined the roan on the edge of the lamplight, and before he could empty his saddle, she ran to him. By the time his boots crunched the grass, she was in his arms.

'Thank God you're safe,' she cried.

'That's more than can be said for Delaney and his gang,' he announced as she clung to him. 'They won't trouble Lonesome Valley again.'

Suddenly she drew in her breath sharply. 'There's blood on your shirt!'

'Just a flesh wound,' he said dismissively. 'Left arm.'

'You come inside, Brett Cassidy,' Harmony stated.

'Sounds like a command,' he said, grinning.

'It sure is and you're obeying!'

Once in the cabin, she helped him shrug out of his bloody shirt. Malloy's bullet had passed right on through, ripping away flesh, but Harmony told him firmly she was going to clean and bandage it. Brett made no protest. He drank the coffee she made him while she sponged his wounded arm. It had been a long time since a woman had touched him like this. A man could get to like this sort of attention.

'This valley owes you so much,' Harmony said as she wrapped the bandage over his wound.

'I just repaid a debt,' he reminded her quietly.

'I hope you're not going to just ride out,' she murmured, tying the bandage.

'I have a home in the mountains,' he reminded her.

'With just yourself for company.' Harmony's hands trailed away from his bandaged arm and covered his. She added in a husky whisper, 'Like me.'

'Two of a kind,' he agreed softly, pulling her on to his lap.

Brett kissed her and she responded passionately, her mouth full of soft promise.

'We have a lot to talk about, Brett,' Harmony said. 'Could take an hour, maybe all night. Could be even longer.' Then she blushed as she blurted out, 'One thing's for sure. You're not going to sleep in the stable.'

'Never intended to, Harmony,' he said.